J.G. Ballard

was born in 1930 in Shanghai, China, where his father was a businessman. Following the attack on Pearl Harbor, he and his family were placed in a civilian prison camp. They returned to England in 1946. After reading Medicine at Cambridge for two years, he worked as a copywriter and Covent Garden porter before going to Canada with the RAF. His first short story appeared in *New Worlds* in 1956, and after working on scientific journals he published his first major novel, *The Drowned World*, in 1962. His acclaimed 1984 novel *Empire of the Sun* won the *Guardian* Fiction Prize and the James Tait Black Memorial Prize, and was shortlisted for the Booker Prize. It was later filmed by Steven Spielberg. His controversial 1973 novel *Crash* has also been made into an equally controversial film, directed by David Cronenberg.

J.G. Ballard's recent novels include *The Kindness of Women*, *Rushing to Paradise* and *Cocaine Nights*. His latest no...l, *Super-Cannes*, is published by Flamingo in autu...

From the reviews of *The Unlimited*...

'I was completely beguiled. . . ...
mastery, it is the most cunning evoc...

Daily Telegraph

'The idea is blindingly original and yet as basic as a dream of the whole human race. Moving, thrilling, exquisitely written.'

ANTHONY BURGESS

'Ballard is one of the few genuine surrealists in business. . . At its most heightened, Ballard's prose is an impacted mass of images, dense and iridescent as mercury, stranger, you might say, than fiction.' *Guardian*

'An extraordinary and touching piece of surrealism . . . [a] strange and beautiful extravaganza.' *Glasgow Herald*

MODERN CLASSIC

J.G. BALLARD

The Unlimited Dream Company

Flamingo
An Imprint of HarperCollins*Publishers*

Flamingo
An Imprint of HarperCollins*Publishers*
77–85 Fulham Palace Road,
Hammersmith, London W6 8JB

Flamingo is a registered trade mark of
HarperCollins Publishers Limited

www.**fire**and**water**.com

A Flamingo Modern Classic 2000
9 8 7 6 5 4 3 2

Previously published in paperback by Flamingo 1992

First published in Great Britain by
Jonathan Cape Ltd 1979

Author photograph by Jerry Bauer

ISBN 0 586 08995 0

Set in Plantin

Printed and bound in Great Britain by
Omnia Books Limited, Glasgow

Contents

CHAPTER 1

The Coming of the Helicopters

In the first place, why did I steal the aircraft?

If I had known that only ten minutes after taking off from London Airport the burning machine was to crash into the Thames, would I still have climbed into its cock-pit? Perhaps even then I had a confused premonition of the strange events that would take place in the hours following my rescue.

As I stand here in the centre of this deserted riverside town I can see my tattered flying suit reflected in the windows of a nearby supermarket, and clearly remember when I entered that unguarded hangar at the airport. Seven days ago my mind was as cool and stressed as the steel roof above my head. While I strapped myself into the pilot's seat I knew that a lifetime's failures and false starts were at last giving way to the simplest and most mysterious of all actions – flight!

Above the film studios helicopters are circling. Soon the police will land on this empty shopping mall, no doubt keen to question me about the disappearance of Shepperton's entire population. I only wish that I could see their surprise when they discover the remarkable way in which I have transformed this peaceful town.

Unsettled by the helicopters, the birds are rising into the air, and I know that it is time for me to leave. Thousands of them surround me, from every corner of the globe, flamingos and frigate-birds, falcons and deep-water albatross, as if sprung from the cages of a well-stocked zoo. They perch on the portico of the filling-station, jostle for a place on the warm roofs of the abandoned cars. When I lean against a pillar-box, trying to straighten my ragged flying suit, the harpy eagle guarding these never-to-be-collected letters snaps at my hands, as if she has forgotten who I am and is curious to

7

inspect this solitary pilot who has casually stepped off the wind into these deserted streets. The barbarous plumage of cockatoos, macaws and scarlet ibis covers the shopping mall, a living train that I would like to fasten around my waist. During the past few minutes, as I made sure that none of my neighbours had been left behind, the centre of Shepperton has become a spectacular aviary, a huge aerial reserve ruled by the condors.

Only the condors will remain with me to the end. Two of these great vultures are watching me now from the concrete roof of the car-park. Fungus stains the tips of their wings, and the pus of decaying flesh glints between their talons, carrion gold shining in the claws of restless money-changers. Like all the birds, they give the impression that they might attack me at any moment, excited by the helicopters and the barely healed wound on my chest.

Despite these suburban pleasantries, I wish that I could stay longer here and come to terms with everything that has happened to me, and the consequences for us all that extend far beyond the boundaries of this small town fifteen miles to the west of London. Around me the streets are silent in the afternoon light. Toys lie by the garden gates, dropped in mid-game by the children when they ran away an hour ago, and one of my neighbours has forgotten to turn off his lawn sprinkler. It rotates tirelessly, casting a succession of immaculate rainbows over the ornamental pond at the foot of the garden, as if hoping to lasso a spectral fish from its deeps.

'Mrs St Cloud . . . ! Father Wingate . . . !' I miss them already, the widow who tried to finance my flying school, and the priest who found my bones in the river bed.

'Miriam . . . ! Dr Miriam . . . !' The young doctor who revived me when I had almost drowned.

All have left me now. Beckoning the birds to follow me, I set off across the shopping mall. On a beach by the river is a hiding place where I can wait until the helicopters have gone. For the last time I look up at the vivid tropical vegetation that forms Shepperton's unique skyline. Orchids and horse-tail ferns crowd the roofs of the supermarket and filling-station, saw-leaved palmettos flourish in the windows of the hardware store and the television rental office, mango trees and magnolia overrun the once sober gardens, transforming this quiet suburban town where I crash-landed only a week ago into some corner of a forgotten Amazon city.

The helicopters are nearer now, clattering up and down the deserted streets by the film studios. The crews peer through their binoculars at the empty houses. But although the townspeople have left, I can still feel their presence within my body. In the window of the appliance store I see my skin glow like an archangel's, lit by the dreams of these housewives and secretaries, film actors and bank cashiers as they sleep within me, safe in the dormitories of my bones.

At the entrance to the park are the memorials which they built to me before they embarked on their last flight. With good-humoured irony, they constructed these shrines from miniature pyramids of dishwashers and television sets, kiosks of record players ornamented with sunflowers, gourds and nectarines, the most fitting materials these suburbanites could find to celebrate their affection for me. Each of these arbours contains a fragment of my flying suit or a small section of the aircraft, a memento of our flights together in the skies above Shepperton, and of that man-powered flying machine I dreamed all my life of building and which they helped me to construct.

One of the helicopters is close behind me, making a tentative circuit of the town centre. Already the pilot and navigator have seen my skin glowing through the trees. But for all their concern, they might as well abandon their machine in mid-air. Soon there will be too many deserted towns for them to count. Along the Thames valley, all over Europe and the Americas, spreading outwards across Asia and Africa, ten thousand similar suburbs will empty as people gather to make their first man-powered flights.

I know now that these quiet, tree-lined roads are runways, waiting for us all to take off for those skies I sought seven days ago when I flew my light aircraft into the air-space of this small town by the Thames, into which I plunged and where I escaped both my death and my life.

CHAPTER 2

I Steal the Aircraft

Dreams of flight haunted that past year.

Throughout the summer I had worked as an aircraft cleaner at London Airport. In spite of the incessant noise and the millions of tourists moving in and out of the terminal buildings I was completely alone. Surrounded by parked airliners, I walked down the empty aisles with my vacuum-cleaner, sweeping away the debris of journeys, the litter of uneaten meals, of unused tranquillizers and contraceptives, memories of arrivals and departures that reminded me of all my own failures to get anywhere.

Already, at the age of twenty-five, I knew that the past ten years of my life had been an avalanche zone. Whatever new course I set myself, however carefully I tried to follow a fresh compass bearing, I flew straight into the nearest brick wall. For some reason I felt that, even in being myself, I was acting a part to which someone else should have been assigned. Only my compulsive role-playing, above all dressing up as a pilot in the white flying suit I found in one of the lockers, touched the corners of some kind of invisible reality.

At seventeen I had been expelled from the last of half a dozen schools. I had always been aggressive and lazy, inclined to regard the adult world as a boring conspiracy of which I wanted no part. As a small child I had been injured in the car crash that killed my mother, and my left shoulder developed a slight upward tilt that I soon exaggerated into a combative swagger. My school-friends liked to mimic me, but I ignored them. I thought of myself as a new species of winged man. I remembered Baudelaire's albatross, hooted at by the crowd, but unable to walk only because of his heavy wings.

11

Everything touched off my imagination in strange ways. The school science library, thanks to an over-enlightened biology master, was a cornucopia of deviant possibilities. In a dictionary of anthropology I discovered a curious but touching fertility rite, in which the aboriginal tribesmen dug a hole in the desert and took turns to copulate with the earth. Powerfully moved by this image, I wandered around in a daze, and one midnight tried to have an orgasm with the school's most cherished cricket pitch. In a glare of torch-beams I was found drunk on the violated turf, surrounded by beer bottles. Strangely enough, the attempt seemed far less bizarre to me than it did to my appalled headmaster.

Expulsion hardly affected me. Since early adolescence I had been certain that one day I would achieve something extraordinary, astonish even myself. I knew the power of my own dreams. Since my mother's death I had been brought up partly by her sister in Toronto and the rest of the time by my father, a successful eye surgeon preoccupied with his practice who never seemed properly to recognize me. In fact, I had spent so much time on transatlantic jets that my only formal education had come from in-flight movies.

After a year at London University I was thrown out of the medical school – while dissecting a thorax in the anatomy laboratory one afternoon I suddenly became convinced that the cadaver was still alive. I terrorized a weak fellow student into helping me to frogmarch the corpse up and down the laboratory in an attempt to revive it. I am still half-certain that we would have succeeded.

Disowned by my father – I had never been close to him and often fantasized that my real father was one of the early American astronauts, and that I had been conceived by semen ripened in outer space, a messianic figure born *into* my mother's womb from a pregnant universe – I began an erratic and increasingly steep slalom. Rejected would-be mercenary pilot, failed Jesuit novice, unpublished writer of pornography (I spent many excited weekends dialling deserted offices all over London and dictating extraordinary sexual fantasies into their answering machines, to be typed out for amazed executives by the unsuspecting secretaries) – yet for all these failures I had a tenacious faith in myself, a messiah as yet without a message who would one day assemble a unique identity out of this defective jigsaw.

For six months I worked in the aviary at London Zoo. The birds drove me mad with their incessant cheeping and chittering, but I learned a great deal from them, and my obsession with man-powered flight began at this point. Once I was arrested by the police for being over-boisterous in the children's playground near the zoo where I spent much of my spare time. For five minutes one rainy afternoon I was gripped by a Pied Piper complex, and genuinely believed that I could lead the twenty children and their startled mothers, the few passing dogs and even the dripping flowers away to a paradise which was literally, if I could only find it, no more than a few hundred yards from us.

Outside the courthouse, where I had been discharged by a sympathetic magistrate, I was befriended by a retired air hostess who now worked as a barmaid at a London Airport hotel and had just been convicted of soliciting at the West London Air Terminal. She was a spirited and likeable girl with a fund of strange stories about the sexual activities at international airports. Carried away by these visions, I immediately proposed to her and moved into the apartment she rented near Heathrow. At this time I was obsessed with the idea of building a man-powered aircraft. Already I was planning the world's first circumnavigation, and saw myself as the Lindbergh and Saint-Exupéry of man-powered flight. I began to visit the airport each day, watching the airliners and the thousands of passengers taking off into the sky. I envied them, their profoundly ordinary lives crossed by this incredible dream of flight.

Flying dreams haunted me more and more. After a few weeks spent on the observation decks I found a job as an aircraft cleaner. On the southern side of London Airport was a section reserved for light aircraft. I spent all my free time in the parking hangars, sitting at the controls of these wind-weary but elegant machines, complex symbols that turned all sorts of keys in my mind. One day, accepting the logic of my dreams, I decided to take off myself.

So began my real life.

Whatever my motives at the time, however, an event that morning had profoundly unsettled me. While watching my fiancée dressing in the bedroom, I felt a sudden need to embrace her. Her uniform was decorated with flying motifs, and I always enjoyed the way she put on this grotesque costume. But as I held her shoulders against my chest I knew that I was not moved by any affection for her but by the need literally to crush her out of existence. I remember the bedside lamp falling to the floor at our feet, knocked down by her flailing arm. As she struck my face with her hard fists I stood by the bed, choking her against my chest. Only when she collapsed around my knees did I realize that I had been about to kill her, but without the slightest hate or anger.

Later, as I sat in the cockpit of the Cessna, excited by the engine as it coughed and thundered into life, I knew that I had meant no harm to her. But at the same time I remembered the dumb fear in her face as she sat on the floor, and I was certain that she would go to the police. Narrowly missing a stationary airliner, I took off on one of the parking runways. I had watched the mechanics start the engines and often badgered them to let me sit beside them as they taxied around the hangars. Several of them were qualified pilots and told me all I needed to know about the flight controls and engine settings. Strangely, now that I was actually airborne, crossing the car-parks, plastics factories and reservoirs that surrounded the airport, I had no idea what course to set. Even then I realized that I would soon be caught and charged with stealing the Cessna after attempting to murder my fiancée.

Forgetting to raise the flaps, I was unable to climb higher than 500 feet, but the idea of low-flying aircraft had always excited me. About five miles south of the airport the engine began to overheat. Within seconds it caught fire and filled the cabin with burning smoke. Below me was a placid riverside town, its tree-lined suburban streets and shopping centre tucked into a wide bend of the river. There were film studios, technicians on a lawn by their cameras. A dozen antique biplanes were drawn up by the canvas mock-up of a camouflaged hangar, and actors in World War I leather flying gear raised their goggles to stare up at me as I soared past, trailing an immense plume of smoke. A man standing on a platform above a metal tower waved his megaphone at me, as if trying to incorporate me into his film.

By now the burning oil that filled the cabin was scorching my face and hands. I decided to put the aircraft down into the river – rather than be burned alive I would drown. Half a mile ahead, beyond tennis courts and a park ringed by dead elms, a large Tudor mansion stood above a sloping lawn that ran down to the water.

As the aircraft crossed the park my shoes were on fire. Vaporizing glycol raced up the funnels of my trousers, scalding my legs and about to boil my testicles. The treetops rushed by on either side. The undercarriage splintered the brittle upper branches of the dead elms, and a cloud of starlings erupted from the trees like shrapnel from a shell. The control column struck itself from my hands. At the last moment I shouted at the river as it rose towards me. Falling apart in the air, its tail impaled by the branches, the aircraft plunged into the water. Spray and steam exploded through the fuselage, the hot pellets striking my face. Hurled forwards against the harness, I felt my head strike the cabin door, but without any sense of pain, as if my body belonged to a passenger.

However, I was certain that I never lost consciousness. Immediately the aircraft began to sink. As I tried to release the harness, struggling with the unfamiliar buckle, a seething black water filled the cabin and swirled in a greedy way around my waist. I knew that within a few seconds I would be drowned.

At this point I saw a vision.

CHAPTER 3
The Vision

Supported by its wings, the aircraft lay passively in the water. A huge cloud of steam rose from the submerged engine and drifted towards the bank. The nose tilted forwards, and the river lapped in an off-hand way at the fractured windshield in front of my face. I slipped the release catch of my harness, and was trying to force open the cabin door when my attention was held by the scene in front of me.

I seemed to be looking at an enormous illuminated painting, lit both by the unsettled water and by a deep light transmitted through the body of the canvas. What surprised me, as I pushed the cabin door against the current, was the intense clarity of every detail. In front of me, above its sloping lawn, was the half-timbered Tudor mansion. A number of people were watching me, like figures posed by the artist in a formal landscape. None of them moved, as if frozen by the burning aircraft that had burst out of the afternoon sky and fallen into the water at their feet.

Although I had never been to this town before – Shepperton, I assumed, from the presence of the film studios – I was convinced that I recognized their faces, and that they were a party of film actors resting between takes. Nearest to me was a dark-haired young woman wearing a white laboratory coat. She stood on the foam-flecked lawn below the mansion, playing in a distracted way with three small children. Two boys and a girl, they sat side by side on a swing like monkeys huddled together on a perch, smiling hopefully at whatever game the young woman was trying to arrange for them. Out of the sides of their eyes they watched me in a knowing way, as if they had been waiting all day for me to land my plane in the water for them. The smaller of the boys wore leg-irons, and whistled now and then at his heavy feet, encouraging them to kick the air. The other boy, a stocky, large-skulled mongol, whispered something to the girl, a pretty child with pale cheeks and secretive eyes.

Above them, in an upstairs window of the mansion, was a handsome, middle-aged woman with a widow's empty face, the mother, I guessed, of the girl in the white coat. She held the brocade curtain in one hand, a forgotten cigarette in the other, unsure whether the violence of my arrival might drag her down with me. She was calling to a bearded man in his late fifties who sat on the narrow beach that separated me from the bank. An archaeologist of some kind, he was surrounded by easel, wicker hamper and specimen trays, his strong but over-weight body squeezed into a small canvas chair. Although his shirt was soaked with water splashed across him by the aircraft, he was staring intently at something on the beach that had caught his attention.

The last of these seven witnesses was a man of about thirty, naked but for his swimming trunks, who stood at the end of a wrought-iron pier jutting into the river from the group of riverside hotels beyond the mansion. He was painting the gondola of a miniature Ferris wheel, part of a children's funfair built on to this crumbling Edwardian pier. He paused paint-brush in hand, and with complete presence of mind glanced casually over his shoulder at me, displaying his blond hair and the showy, muscular physique of a film company athlete.

The water rose around my chest, surging through the submerged dials of the instrument panel. I waited for one of the witnesses to come to my help, but they stood like actors waiting for a director's cue, their figures lit by the vibrant light that suffused the air. A deep, premonitory glow lay over the mansion, the amusement pier and the hotels by the marina, as if in the last micro-seconds before an immense disaster. I was almost convinced that a huge airliner had

18

crashed on to this suburban town or that it was about to be overwhelmed by a nuclear catastrophe.

The river swirled across the windshield. A murky foam thrashed against the fractured glass. At the last moment I saw the archaeologist rise from his chair, strong arms outstretched across the water, trying to will me from the aircraft as if he had suddenly realized his responsibility for me.

The starboard wing sank below the surface. Dragged by the current, the Cessna rolled on to its side. Breaking free from my harness, I forced back the door and clambered from the flooded cabin on to the port wing strut. I climbed on to the roof and stood there in my ragged flying suit as the aircraft sank below me into the water, taking my dreams and hopes into its deep.

CHAPTER 4

An Attempt to Kill Me

I was lying on the wet grass below the mansion. People jostled around me in what seemed to be a drunken brawl, ordered back by the young woman in the white coat.

'Dr Miriam –!'

'I can see he isn't dead! Now get away!' She brushed her untidy hair out of her eyes and knelt beside me, a nervous but strong hand on my breast-bone, ready to pump my heart back to life. 'Good God . . . you seem to be all right.'

For all the authority in this young woman's voice, she was totally confused by something, still not altogether sure that I was alive. Behind her was the middle-aged woman I had seen in the window of the mansion. She stared at me in an appalled way, as if she, and not I, had escaped from the accident. Engine grease marked her silk blouse and the pearls hanging from her neck. She held the forgotten cigarette in her left hand, about to brand this drenched aviator who had wrestled himself on to the grass.

She reached down and angrily shook my shoulder.

'Who *are* you!'

'Mrs St Cloud! You'll hurt him, madam . . . !'

A man in chauffeur's uniform tried to calm her, but she clung to me in a disorientated way, as if I had stolen something valuable from her.

'Mother!' The young doctor struck her hand from my shoulder. 'He can't cope with you as well! Bring my case from the house!'

The people around me stepped back reluctantly, revealing a placid sky. The intense light had gone, and the Ferris wheel rotated against the clouds like an amiable mandala. I felt strong but strangely old, as if I had completed an immense voyage. I touched the doctor's arm in an effort to calm her, wondering how to warn her of the disaster about to overwhelm this small town.

She patted my cheek reassuringly. Obviously she had been deeply impressed by the dramatic style of my arrival. Looking up at this confused young woman, I felt a powerful sense of gratitude to her. I wanted to stroke her skin, place my mouth against her breast. For a moment I almost believed that I was her suitor, and that I had chosen this extravagant method of arrival in order to propose marriage to her.

As if aware of this, she smiled and pressed my hand. 'Are you all right? I don't mind saying that you gave me a hell of a scare ... Can you see me? And hear me? How many fingers? Good. Now, was there anyone else in the plane? A passenger?'

'I ... ' For no clear reason I decided not to speak. The image of the Cessna's cockpit formed a blank zone in my mind. I could no longer remember myself at the controls. 'No ... I was alone.'

'You don't sound very sure. Who are you, anyway? You look as if you might forget at any moment.'

'Blake – I'm a stunt pilot. The aircraft caught fire.'

'It certainly did ... '

Taking her arm, I sat up. The wet grass was stained with oil from my flying suit. My shoes were charred, but luckily neither of my feet had been burned. From the respectful faces of the people around me – a gardener, the chauffeur, and an elderly couple who appeared to be housekeepers – I knew they had all assumed that I had drowned and were stunned by my apparent return from the dead. Along the river people were standing by both banks. Tennis players carrying their rackets moved through the trees, and a group of small boys were throwing clods of earth into the water, imitating the aircraft's splash.

The Cessna had vanished in the current, swept away by the dark water.

The archaeologist strode up from the beach, his beard and parson's collar soaked with water. As he caught his breath, staring impatiently at the oil-stained lawn, he resembled a harassed marine prophet come ashore to search for a renegade member of his flock. He gazed at me in a curiously disappointed way. I guessed that he had waded into the river to pull me to safety, assumed like the others that I had died and was about to read the last rites over me.

'Father Wingate – he's come round.' Dr Miriam steadied me against her shoulder. 'That's one miracle I concede to you.'

'I can see that, Miriam.' The priest made no attempt to come any nearer, as if wary of me, rebuffed by my return to the living. 'Well, thank God ... But let him rest.'

The light faded, and then grew suddenly brighter. The priest's face swam, its firm and spartan features leaking across the air into an angry grimace. Exhausted, I leaned against Dr Miriam and laid my head across her warm lap.

I could feel the imprint of a strange mouth against my own. My lips were swollen and cut against my teeth. A pair of powerful hands had bruised themselves into my chest. Whoever had given artificial respiration to me had used unnecessary strength, forcing his fingers between my ribs, as if determined to kill me. Through the deep glare that illuminated the river, now an almost lunar domain without shadows, I could see the priest watching me with a peculiar intensity, as if he were challenging me in some way. Had he tried to revive me, or kill me?

At the same time, I knew that I had not lost consciousness. I remembered stepping from the roof of the aircraft and swimming strongly for the shore, and then being steered by someone through the shallows. I looked up at the sky, which hovered on the verge of that vivid glow I had seen from the cockpit of the Cessna. As Dr Miriam held my head in her lap, her fingers pressed anxiously to my temples, I was about to warn her of the disaster.

Abruptly, the sky cleared. Dr Miriam was looking at me in a reflective way, as if we were lovers long familiar with each other's bodies. I could smell her strong thighs, and see her surprisingly grimy feet within their sandals. Her untidy hair was tied back in a faded ribbon. Through a missing button of her blouse I stared at a child's scratch-marks on her left breast. I wanted to embrace her, here on this open lawn in front of this aggressive priest. I was sure that the violence of my accident had aroused her, and I was disappointed that it was not her mouth that had cut my lips.

She checked herself, and began wiping the oil from my face with a scented handkerchief. At any moment the local police would arrive, drawn by the crowd watching along the bank. Hundreds of people were staring at me across the calm water.

I stood up and leaned against the swing, while the three children watched me from their perch. They laughed hysterically when I kicked the charred shoes from my feet. The flying suit hung in rags around my waist. The right shoulder and leg were missing, torn from me as I escaped from the Cessna.

Turning my back on the priest, I said: 'I have to leave. I'm an instructor at a flying school – they'll need to know the aircraft came down here.'

'I thought you were a stunt pilot.'

'I am, in a way. I am a stunt pilot.' To avoid her interested gaze, I asked: 'What's the matter with your mother? She's mad . . .'

'You startled her, to put it mildly. Now, wait a minute.' She stood in front of me and felt my bruised ribs and abdomen, like a teacher inspecting a child injured in a playground. The blood from my grazed knuckles spotted her hands. Once again I felt a strong sexual attraction to her, part of my nervous relief at being alive. There was a slight swelling under her upper lip, as if she had bruised it kissing her lover.

23

'Before you leave I want to take an X-ray of that head. Five minutes ago we thought you'd . . . '

She left the sentence unfinished, less out of deference to me than to the clergyman. He had moved a few steps closer but had still not joined us. His level stare made me sure that he already suspected I was not a qualified pilot.

Dr Miriam squeezed the water from my suit. 'Father Wingate, who's the patron saint of stunt pilots and flying instructors? There must be one.'

'Clearly there must be. Miriam, leave the poor fellow alone.' To me, he added: 'It isn't every day that young men fall from the sky.'

'More's the pity.' She turned from me and silenced the three children, who were running around the swing. The boy with leg-irons was uttering a series of whooping cries that sounded like a parody of my voice. 'Jamie – why are you being cruel?'

I thought of clouting the boy but the priest touched my shoulder. He had at last approached me, and was staring into my face as if reading the seams in one of his bone-beds. 'Before you go. You're all right, are you? You must have a powerful will – you literally came to life in our hands.'

For all his pious tone, I knew that he was not about to ask me to join him in a prayer of thanks. My apparent return from the dead had clearly shaken the orders and proprieties of his universe. Perhaps he had tried to revive me on the beach, and after all these years of wearing the cloth was embarrassed to find that he had apparently performed a miracle.

Seeing his strong physique at close quarters, the shoulders still trembling with some strange repressed emotion, I could easily imagine him deciding to crush the life out of me and send me back to the other side before everything got out of hand. He was deliberately exposing the suspicions that crossed his face, trying to provoke me. I was tempted to grapple with him, force my bruised body against his and hurl him on to the oil-stained grass.

I touched my lips, wondering if the priest had revived me by this act of oral rape. Someone with powerful arms had crushed the air from my lungs – a man of my own size, judging from the imprint of his mouth and hands. The priest was old enough to be my father, but despite his dog-collar he had the aggressive physique of a rugby player.

I looked at the circle of faces, at the people lining the opposite bank of the river. If not the priest, then which of the seven witnesses? Perhaps Dr Miriam, or her dotty mother. Mrs St Cloud had emerged from the mansion, the oil-stained pearls hanging in a greasy chain around her neck. She still hesitated to approach me, as if she expected me to ignite spontaneously and destroy her already disfigured lawn.

The last of the witnesses, the blond-haired man painting the Ferris wheel, had stepped down from the rusting pier and was now walking along the beach towards us. He strolled through the shallow water in his bare feet, showing off his almost naked body to me. His casual paddling had a serious purpose, re-establishing his rights over this water I had temporarily made my own.

He waved to Dr Miriam, the small conspiratorial gesture of a past lover, waiting for her to invite him on to the lawn. When she ignored him he pointed in an off-hand but sly way to the dead elms above our heads.

Looking up, I saw a section of the Cessna's tail suspended from the upper branches. Pinned against the sky, it flicked from side to side, a flag already semaphoring my presence to the searching police.

'Stark . . . he's always had sharp eyes.' As if protecting me, Dr Miriam took my arm. 'Blake, come on. We ought to leave. I'll find you something to wear at the clinic.'

At that time, as I followed her across the lawn, I was aware only of the silent crowd watching me from both banks of the river, the tennis players sitting with their rackets on the grass. Their faces seemed almost hostile. Seen through this strange light, the placid town into which I had fallen had a distinctly sinister atmosphere, as if all these apparently unhurried suburbanites were in fact actors recruited from the film studios to play their roles in an elaborate conspiracy.

We reached Dr Miriam's sports car in the drive behind the house. Hovering in the porch, Mrs St Cloud handed the medical bag to her daughter.

'Miriam – ?'

'Mother, for heaven's sake. I'll be quite safe.' With a tolerant shake of her head, Dr Miriam opened the car door for me.

As I stood there barefoot in the oil-stained rags of my flying suit I was suddenly certain that Mrs St Cloud would not run to the telephone the moment I left. This middle-aged widow had never seen anyone return from the dead. With a hand to her throat, she stared at me as if I were a son whose existence she had absent-mindedly misplaced.

At the same time, I had no intention of outstaying my welcome. For whatever motives, one of these people had tried to kill me.

CHAPTER 5

Back from the Dead

Should I have been more wary of Miriam St Cloud? Even then, as we approached the clinic, it seemed strange that I was so ready to trust this young doctor. Little more than a student, with her white coat and grass-stained feet, she sat seriously over the wheel. She was still unsettled, putting herself to unnecessary trouble to look after me, and I suspected that she might try to drive me to the local police station. We stopped several times under the trees, giving the three children time to catch up with us. They raced across the park, whooping and hooting, as if hoping to shock the solemn beeches out of their silence. I kept a careful watch for the arrival of the police, my arm behind Dr Miriam's seat. If a patrol car appeared I was ready to wrest the controls from her and bundle her out on to the grass.

The sunlight shivered through the trees. The birds and leaves were restive, as if the elements of the disrupted afternoon were trying to reconstitute themselves.

'Do you want to go back to your mother?' I asked. 'I'd say she needs you more than I do.'

'You upset her – she wasn't expecting you to recover so dramatically. Since father's death two years ago she's spent all her time by the window, almost as if he were out here somewhere. Next time you come back from the dead do it in easy stages.'

'I didn't come *back* from the dead.'

'Blake, I know . . . ' Annoyed with herself, she pressed my hand. I liked this young doctor, but her light-hearted reference to my death irritated me, a touch of dissecting-room humour I could do without. In fact, apart from my bruised mouth and ribs, I felt remarkably well. I remembered swimming strongly for the shore as the Cessna sank beneath me, and then fainting in the shallows, more from relief than real exhaustion. The clergyman had pulled me on to the grass, and at this point in the confusion some lunatic had tried to revive me, some half-trained suburban first-aid enthusiast. Already I resolved that the sooner I left Shepperton the better, before any other blunder could occur.

However, before I could leave I needed a new set of clothes.

'There's a spare suit at the clinic, though your pupils at the flying school won't recognize you in it.' She added in a droll way: 'I'm deliberately being cryptic – you might decide to jump out of this car.'

'As long as the suit didn't belong to someone who died. Tempting providence twice the same afternoon isn't the kind of thing your priest would approve of.'

'Blake, you didn't tempt providence.' Choosing her words, she went on matter-of-factly: 'Actually, people don't die at the clinic, it's for out-patients only. Believe me, I'm glad you weren't our first recruit. There's a geriatric unit attached to it – the three children are temporarily there on referral, no one else would take them. I'm sorry they were being silly, but before they came here they'd been terribly abused.'

She pointed to a three-storey building beyond the clinic's car-park. On the terrace a line of elderly patients sat in their wheelchairs, nodding at the sun. As soon as they saw my ragged flying suit they immediately revived, began to point at me and argue with each other. I assumed that they had seen the burning Cessna fly over and hit the trees along the river.

We waited in the car-park for the three children to run up to us. Unaware that I was watching her closely, Dr Miriam leaned against one of the cars and picked at a fleck of dirt under her thumbnail. For some reason, perhaps the heat reflected from the polished cellulose and my own half-naked body, I felt suddenly obsessed with this young woman, with the chipped varnish on her toe-nails, the grass-stains on her heels, the heady smell of her thighs and armpits, and even the cryptic residue of some patient's bodily functions on her white coat. She flicked the dirt from her nail on to the grass, as if returning to the park part of that bountiful nature welling up ceaselessly through her pores. I felt that her grubby feet and air of untidiness stemmed not from any lack of hygiene but from her complete absorption in all the commonplaces of nature. I knew that she cured her patients with poultices of earth and spit, rolled together in her strong hands and warmed between her thighs. Infatuated with her smell, I wanted to mount her like a stallion taking a meadow-rich mare.

'Blake . . . ?' She was watching me in a not unfriendly way, as if she knew that I was no ordinary pilot and was deliberately letting herself be attracted to me. When the children reached us she bent down and embraced them warmly in turn, smiling unflinchingly when the little girl's sticky fingers searched her mouth.

The child was blind. I realized now why these three handicapped children stayed so close – in this way they pooled their abilities. The girl was the brightest of the trio, with an alert, pointed face and a lively, questing nose. The larger of the two boys, the stocky mongol with his massive forehead like an air-raid shelter, was her devoted guide-dog, always within hands'-reach and careful to steer her between the parked cars. He kept up a continuous murmured commentary on everything, presenting to his blind companion what must have been the picture of a dream-like and affable world.

The third child was a small, sandy-haired boy who squinted at the sky with tremendous excitement as if rediscovering each second the sheer joy of all that went on around him. As he gazed at the sun-filled park every leaf and flower seemed to hold the promise of a special treat. He used the leg-iron shackled to his right foot as a pivot, swinging around on it with some style.

I watched them scuttle around me, in and out of the cars. I liked this self-reliant threesome, and wished that I could help them. I remembered my Pied Piper complex. Somewhere in this park there might well be a miniature paradise, a secret domain where I could give the blind girl her sight, strong legs to the spastic, intelligence to the mongol.

'What is it, Rachel . . . ?' Dr Miriam bent down to catch her whisper. 'Rachel's very keen to know what you look like. I haven't quite convinced her that you're not a personal messenger from the archangel Michael.'

The girl's agile hands, with their acute flexion at the wrists, were already tracing out the contours of a face. Like the two boys, she seemed to cross reality at an angle. I lifted her and held her against my chest, partly to confirm that her small hands could not have bruised my ribs. Her thin breath panted into my face as her fingers raced like excited moths over my cheeks and forehead, poked into my mouth and nostrils. I almost enjoyed the sharp pain as she touched my lips. I held her tightly, squeezing her hips against my abdomen.

The mongol was tugging at my wrists, alarmed eyes under his overloaded forehead. The girl cried out, shaking her blind face away from my lips.

'Blake! Put her down!' Dr Miriam pulled the child from my arms. She stared at me in a shocked way, unsure whether this was how I ordinarily behaved. Fifty yards away, Father Wingate was crossing the park. He had stopped under the trees, the canvas chair and wicker hamper in his strong hands, watching me as if I were some kind of escaped criminal. I knew that he had seen me seize the girl.

Dr Miriam lowered the child to the ground. 'David, Jamie – take Rachel with you.'

The girl tottered away from me, safe within the mongol's protective gaze. Clearly he was unable to decide whether Rachel had really been frightened by me. They ran off into the park together. Rachel's hands were tracing out the profiles of some extraordinary face.

'What did she see?'

'By the looks of it, a kind of bizarre bird.'

Dr Miriam stood between me and the children, making sure that I did not take it into my head to run after them. My arms were still shaking from the effort of embracing the child. I knew that Dr Miriam was well aware of the brief sexual frenzy that had gripped me, and half-expected me to wrestle her into the back seat of the nearest car. How fiercely would she have fought me off? She stayed close to me when we entered the clinic, wary that I might assault one of the elderly patients shuffling into the waiting room.

But once we were in her office she deliberately turned her back to me, almost inviting me to hold her waist. She was still confused by the excitement of my crash-landing. For all her modesty, as she listened to my heart and lungs her hands never left me. I watched her in an almost dream-like way while she pressed my shoulders against the X-ray machine. The exquisite mole like a beautiful cancer below her left ear, the handsome black hair swept back out of harm's way, the unsettled eyes ruled by her high forehead, the blue vein in her temple that pulsed with some kind of erratic emotion – I wanted to examine all these at my leisure, savour the scent of her armpits, save for ever in a phial hung around my neck the tag of loose skin on her lip. Far from being a stranger, I felt that I had known her for years.

She brought me the spare suit she had promised and watched me while I changed, staring frankly at my naked body and half-erect penis. I pulled on the black worsted trousers and jacket, the dry-cleaned suit of a priest or funeral mute, fitted with unusual pockets designed to conceal a secret rosary or the bereaved's tips.

When she returned with the developed X-ray plates she handed me a pair of tennis shoes.

'I'll look like an undertaker out for a quiet run.' I waited as she examined these photographs of my skull. 'For a year I was a medical student. Who owns the copyright? They may be valuable.'

'We do. They probably are. Thank God there's nothing there. Will you come back for the aeroplane?'

I paused at the door, glad that she wanted to see me again. Avoiding my eyes, she was gently rubbing her fingers, stroking the faint traces of my skin. But was all this some kind of unconscious ruse? I knew that I had identified this young doctor with my safe escape from the Cessna. How far was my attraction to her self-serving, the grave's-love of an infatuated patient? All the same, I wanted to warn her of the danger threatening this small town. However grotesque, my vision of the imminent holocaust had gained a powerful conviction in my mind. Perhaps in moments of extreme crisis we stepped outside the planes of everyday time and space and were able to catch a glimpse of all events that had ever occurred in both past and future.

'Miriam, wait. Before I go . . . has there ever been a major disaster in Shepperton? A factory explosion, or a crashing airliner?'

When she shook her head, looking at me with a suddenly professional interest, I pointed through the window at the calm sky, at the park filled with bland summer light where the crippled children played, circling each other like aircraft with outstretched arms. 'After the crash I had a premonition that there was going to be some kind of disaster – perhaps even a nuclear accident. There was an enormous glow in the sky, an intense light. Come with me . . . ' I tried to take her arm. 'I'll look after you.'

She placed her hands on my chest, her fingers overlaying the bruise-marks. She had not revived me. 'It's nothing, Blake, nothing unusual. It's common for the dying to see bright lights. At the end the brain tries to rally itself, to free itself from the body. I suppose it's where we get our ideas of the soul.'

'I wasn't dying!' Her fingers stung my ribs. I was tempted to seize her by the neck, force her to take a long look at my still erect penis. 'Miriam, look at me – I swam from the aircraft!'

'Yes, you did, Blake. We saw you.' She touched me again, reminding herself that I was still with her. Confused by her feelings for me, she said: 'Blake, while you were trapped in the cockpit I actually prayed for you. We weren't sure you were alone. Just before you escaped there seemed to be two people there.'

I remembered the deep light that suffused the air above the town, as if some fiercely incandescent vapour had been about to ignite. Had there been someone else in the Cessna's cockpit? Just beyond the margin of my vision there seemed to be the figure of a seated man.

'I swam from the aircraft,' I repeated doggedly. 'Some fool gave me artificial respiration. Who was it!'

'No one. I'm certain.' She straightened the clutter of pens on her desk, so many confusing pointers, watching me with the same expression I had seen on her mother's face. I realized that she was attracted to me but at the same time almost disgusted, as if fascinated by something in an open grave.

'Miriam . . . ' I wanted to reassure her.

But in a sudden access of lucidity she came towards me, buttoning her white coat.

'Blake, haven't you grasped yet what happened?' She stared into my eyes, willing a dull pupil to get the point. 'When you were trapped in the cockpit you were under

33

water for more than eleven minutes. We all thought you'd died.'

'Had I?'

'Yes!' Almost shouting, she angrily struck my hand. 'You *died* . . . ! And then came alive again!'

CHAPTER 6

Trapped by the Motorway

'The girl's mad!'

I slammed the clinic door behind me.

Across the park a white flag signalled an urgent message. The section of the Cessna's tailplane hung from the upper boughs of the dead elm, whipped to and fro by the wind. Fortunately the police had still failed to find me, and none of the tennis players was showing any interest in the downed aircraft. I drummed my fists on the roofs of the parked cars, annoyed with Miriam St Cloud – this likeable but confused woman doctor showed all the signs of turning into a witch. I decided to lose myself among the afternoon housewives and catch the first bus back to the airport.

At the same time I found that I was laughing out loud at myself – the abortive flight had been a double fiasco. Not only had I crashed and nearly killed myself, but the few witnesses who might have tried to save me had developed a vested interest in believing that I had died. The notion of my death in some deranged way fulfilled a profound need, perhaps linked with their sterile lives in this suffocating town – anyone who came within its clutches was unconsciously assumed to have 'died'.

Thinking of Dr Miriam – I would have liked to show her just how dead I was, and seed a child between those shy hips – I strode past the war memorial and open-air swimming-pool. The town centre consisted of little more than a supermarket and shopping mall, a multi-storey car-park and filling station. Shepperton, known to me only for its film studios, seemed to be the everywhere of suburbia, the paradigm of nowhere. Young mothers steered small children in and out of the launderette and supermarket, refuelled their cars at the filling-station. They gazed at their reflections in the appliance-store windows, exposing their handsome bodies to these washing machines and television sets as if setting up clandestine liaisons with them.

As I stared at this array of thighs and breasts I was aware of my nervous sex, set off by the crash, by Miriam St Cloud and the blind child. All my senses seemed to be magnified – scents collided in the air, the shop-fronts flashed gaudy signs at me. I was moving among these young women with my loins at more than half cock, ready to mount them among the pyramids of detergent packs and free cosmetic offers.

Over my head the sky brightened, bathing the placid roofs in an auroral light, transforming this suburban high street into an avenue of temples. I felt queasy and leaned against the chestnut tree outside the post office. I waited for this retinal illusion to pass, unsure whether to halt the passing traffic and warn these ruminating women that they and their offspring were about to be annihilated. Already I was attracting attention. A group of teenagers stopped as I blinked and clenched my fists. They laughed at my grotesque costume, the priest's shiny black suit and the white sneakers.

'Blake – wait for me!'

As I swayed helplessly, surrounded by these tittering youths, I heard Father Wingate shouting at me. He crossed the street, holding back the cars with a strong hand, his forehead glaring like a helmet in the overbright air. He ordered the teenagers away and then stared at me with the same expression of concern and anger, as if I were some deviant usurper he was bound by a strange tie to assist.

'Blake, what are you looking at? Blake –!'

Trying to escape the light, and this odd clergyman, I jumped an ornamental rail and ran off down the side-street of sedate bungalows behind the post office. Father Wingate's voice faded behind me, lost among the car horns and overhead aircraft. Here everything was calmer. The pavements were deserted, the well-tended gardens like miniature memorial parks consecrated to the household gods of the television set and dishwasher.

The light faded as I reached the northern outskirts of the town. Two hundred yards beyond an untilled field ran the broad deck of the motorway. A convoy of trucks was turning off into the nearby exit ramp, each pulling a large trailer that carried a wood and canvas replica of an antique aircraft. As this caravan of aerial fantasies entered the gates of the film studios, dusty dreams of my own flight, I crossed the perimeter road and set off for the pedestrian bridge that spanned the motorway. Poppies and yellow broom brushed my legs, hopefully leaving their pollen on me. They flowered among the debris of worn tyres and abandoned mattresses. To my right was a furniture hypermarket, its open courtyard packed with three-piece suites, dining-tables and wardrobes, through which a few customers moved in an abstracted way, like spectators in a boring museum. Next to the hypermarket was an automobile repair yard, its forecourt filled with used cars. They sat in the sunlight with numerals on their windshields, the advance guard of a digital universe in which everything would be tagged and numbered, a doomsday catalogue listing each stone and grain of sand under my feet, each eager poppy.

Now that I was at last escaping from Shepperton – within moments I would cross the bridge and catch the bus to the airport – I felt confident and light-footed, skipping along in my white sneakers. I paused by a concrete post embedded in the soil, a digit marking this waste land. Looking back for the last time at this stifling town where I had nearly lost my life, I thought of returning to it one night and aerosolling a million ascending numbers on every garden gate, super-market trolley and baby's forehead.

Carried away by this extravaganza, I ran along, shouting numbers at everything around me, at the drivers on the motorway, the modest clouds in the sky, the hangar-like sound stages of the film studios. Already, despite the crash, I was thinking of my new career in aviation – a course of lessons at a flying school, a commission in the air force, I would either bring off the world's first man-powered circumnavigation or become the first European astronaut . . .

Out of breath, I unbuttoned the clerical jacket, about to throw it aside. It was then, fifty yards from the motorway, that I made an unsettling discovery. Although I was walking at a steady pace across the uneven soil, I was no longer drawing any closer to the pedestrian bridge. The sandy ground moved past me, the poppies swayed more urgently against my pollen-covered knees, but the motorway remained as far away as ever. If anything, this distance between us seemed to enlarge. At the same time, Shepperton receded behind me, and I found myself standing in an immense field filled with poppies and a few worn tyres.

I watched the cars speed along the motorway, the faces of their drivers clearly visible. In a sudden sprint, trying to confuse and overrun whatever deranged sense of direction had taken root in my mind, I darted forward and then swerved behind a line of rusting fuel drums.

Again the motorway receded further from me.

Gasping at the dusty air, I stared down at my feet. Had Miriam St Cloud deliberately given me this defective pair of running shoes, part of her witch's repertory?

I carefully tested myself against the silent ground. Around me the waste land remained as I had found it, yielding and unyielding, in league with the secret people of Shepperton. Foxglove grew through the rusting doors of a small car. An unvarying light calmed the waiting nettles along the motorway palisade. A few drivers watched me from their cars, demented priest in my white sneakers. I picked up a chalky stone and set out a line of numbered stakes with pieces of driftwood, a calibrated pathway that would carry me to the pedestrian bridge. But as I walked forward they encircled me in a spiral arm that curved back upon itself, a whorl of numerals that returned me to the centre of the field.

Half an hour later I gave up and walked back to Shepperton. I had exhausted all the stratagems I could devise – crawling, running backwards, shutting my eyes and hand-holding my way along the air. As I left behind the derelict car and the old tyres the streets of the town approached me, as if glad to see me again.

Calming myself, I stepped on to the perimeter road. Clearly the crash had dislocated my head in more ways than I realized. Outside the hypermarket I picked an overstuffed sofa and lay back in the hot sunlight, resting among the reproduction fakes and discount escritoires until I was moved on my way by the wary salesman.

I walked through the garage forecourt, where the burnished cellulose of the second-hand cars glowed in the sun, a line of coloured headaches. Straightening my dusty suit, I set off along the perimeter road. Two women stood with their children by the bus stop. They watched me carefully, as if frightened that I might perform my dervish dance, surround them with hundreds of numbered stakes.

I waited for the bus to appear. I ignored the women's sly glances, but I was tempted to expose myself, let them see my half-erect penis. For someone who was supposed to have died I felt more alive than ever before.

'Don't take your children to Dr Miriam!' I shouted to them. 'She'll tell you they're dead! You see this bright light? It's your minds trying to rally themselves!'

Dizzy with my own sex, I sat down on the kerb by the bus stop, laughing to myself. In the strong afternoon light the deserted road had become a dusty tunnel, a tube of constricting mental pressure. The women watched me, gorgons in summer dresses, their children staring open-mouthed.

Suddenly I was certain that the bus would never come.

The police car crossed the motorway, cruising with its

headlamps full on in the bright sunlight. The beams flared against my bruised skin. Unable to face them, I turned and ran away down the perimeter road.

Already I had begun to realize that Shepperton had trapped me.

CHAPTER 7
Stark's Zoo

A cool stream ran between the poplars, waiting to balm and soothe my skin. Beyond the water-meadow there were yachts and power cruisers moored along the river banks. For ten minutes I had been following the perimeter road, waiting for the right moment to make a second attempt to escape from Shepperton. Lined with chestnut and plane trees, the quiet streets of bungalows and small houses formed a series of green arbours, the entrances to a friendly labyrinth. Here and there a diving board rose above the hedges. Small swimming pools sat in the gardens, water sparkling flintily as if angry at being confined within these domesticated tanks, confused by these obsessively angled floors into which it had been lovingly decanted. I visualized these pools, plagued by small children and their lazy mothers, secretly planning their revenge.

It was plainly not by chance that I had crash-landed my burning aircraft into this riverside town. On all sides Shepperton was surrounded by water – gravel lakes and reservoirs, the settling beds, canals and conduits of the local water authority, the divided arms of the river fed by a maze of creeks and streams. The high embankments of the reservoirs formed a series of raised horizons, and I realized that I was wandering through a marine world. The dappled light below the trees fell upon an ocean floor. Unknown to themselves, these modest suburbanites were exotic marine creatures with the dream-filled minds of aquatic mammals. Around these placid housewives with their tamed appliances everything was suspended in a profound calm. Perhaps the glimmer of threatening light I had seen over Shepperton was a premonitory reflection of this drowned suburban town?

I had reached the hotels near the marina. High above the St Clouds' Tudor mansion the tailplane of the Cessna hung from the dead elm, signalling intermittently as if already bored with its message.

I crossed the road and approached the untended ticket kiosk of the amusement pier. The freshly painted gondolas of the Ferris wheel, the unicorns and winged horses of the miniature carousel gleamed hopefully in the afternoon light, but I guessed that the only people who came to this dilapidated funfair were a few midnight couples.

Behind the kiosk were the almost empty cages of a modest zoo. Two threadbare vultures sat in their hutch, ignoring a dead rabbit on the floor, dreams of the Andes lost behind their sealed eyes. A marmoset slept on his shelf, and an elderly chimpanzee endlessly groomed himself, sensitive fingernails searching his navel as if trying to pick the combination of this umbilical lock, ever-hopeful internal émigré.

As I gazed consolingly at his gentle face a large and flamboyantly decorated vehicle emerged from the gates of the film studios, set off rapidly down the road in a dusty clatter and swerved into the forecourt by the ticket kiosk. A hearse converted to carry surf-board and hang-gliding equipment, it was emblazoned with winged emblems and gilded fish. The blond-haired man who had been painting the gondolas stared at me in a self-conscious way from behind the steering wheel, then pulled off an antique flying helmet. He stepped from the vehicle and busied himself in the ticket kiosk, affecting not to notice me.

However, when I walked out to the end of the pier I heard his feet ringing on the metal slats.

'Blake . . . be careful there!' He waved me away from the flimsy rail, fearing that his rusting hulk might collapse under us. 'Are you all right? This is where you came down.'

He looked at me with some sympathy, but at the same time he stood well back from me, as if at any moment I might do something bizarre. Had he watched my attempt to cross the motorway?

'That was a spectacular landing ... ' He stared at the strong current flowing below our feet. 'I know you're a stunt pilot, but you must have been rehearsing that for years.'

'You're a fool!' I wanted to hit him. 'I nearly killed myself!'

'Blake, I know! I'm sorry – but I suppose we rehearse that too ... ' He played with the antique goggles and helmet, suddenly embarrassed by this rival show of flying gear. 'I'm working on a picture at the studios – the remake of *Men with Wings*. I play one of the test pilots.' He gestured deprecatingly at the Ferris wheel. 'All this is a long-term investment, or was meant to be. It needs something to give it a lift. In fact, I'm surprised more people aren't here this afternoon. It's rather funny, Blake, that you're the only one who's come ... '

He reached up to one of the gondolas and swung himself into the air, showing off his muscular physique not so much to intimidate me – I could have knocked him down without any effort – as to win some kind of physical respect. His manner was aggressive but ingratiating, his mind already hard at work trying to think up some means of putting my crash to his advantage. As he gazed wistfully at the river, at the vanished traces of my accident swept away by the sunlit back of the Thames, I could see that he regretted being unable to exploit the derelict pier's chance proximity to my crash-landing.

'Stark, tell me – you saw me swim ashore?'

'Of course.' As if to forestall any criticism of his lack of action, he explained hurriedly: 'I was going to dive in, Blake, but suddenly there you were, somehow you'd climbed out of the plane.'

'Father Wingate helped me on to the beach. Did you see anyone try to revive me? Mouth to mouth respiration...?'

'No – why do you ask?' Stark was peering at me with a

surprising look of intelligence in his actor's face. 'Don't you remember, Blake?'

'I'd like to thank him, whoever it was.' Casually, I added: 'How long was I in the aircraft?'

Stark was listening to the restive vultures in their cage. The huge birds were clambering around the bars, trying to seize a piece of the sky. I studied Stark's unsettled eyes, the fine hairs that stood like needles around his lips. Had he revived me? I visualized his handsome mouth locked against my own, strong teeth cutting my gums. In many ways Stark resembled a muscular, blond-haired woman. I felt attracted to him, not by some deviant homosexual urge the crash had jerked loose from my psyche, but by an almost brotherly intimacy with his body, with his thighs and shoulders, arms and buttocks, as if we had shared a bedroom through our childhoods. I was the younger but stronger brother, the yardstick against which Stark would for ever measure himself. I could embrace him whenever I chose, force his hands against my bruised ribs to see if he had tried to attack me, test the bite of his mouth.

Confused by my stare, Stark turned his back on the river. 'How long were you under? Three or four minutes. Perhaps more.'

'Ten minutes?'

'That's a long time, Blake. You'd hardly be here.' His composure returned, he watched me shrewdly, curious to see what I would do next. He played with the antique flying helmet, dangling this film prop in front of me as if toying with the suspicion that we were both actor-pilots. Yet I had flown a real plane against the sky, a powered aircraft, not one of his passive hang-gliders collaborating with the wind.

Along the perimeter road the police car approached, headlamps inflaming the afternoon sunlight. When it stopped by the kiosk I saw that Father Wingate was sitting in the rear seat behind the two policemen. He stared at me

44

through the closed window with the pensive gaze of someone who had quietly turned himself in to the police.

As I waited for him to point me out to the officers Stark took my arm. 'Blake, I'm driving to London – I'll give you a lift across the river.'

I sat in the passenger seat of the hearse, wearing my funeral mute's costume, hiding my face behind the folded canopy of the hang-glider. I listened to the chittering of the marmoset, the guttural screeching of the vultures. For some reason my arrival had frayed their nerves. In the rear-view mirror I could see Father Wingate watching me from the back seat of the police car, like a fellow conspirator keeping his own counsel, careful to give away nothing of his involvement with me.

Stark stood by the kiosk with the two policemen, warning them away from the rusty pier and shrugging as they pointed to the sky above the film studios.

So the police were still searching for a witness. As I watched the film actor shake his head I was convinced that despite all the uncertainties of the afternoon neither Stark nor Father Wingate, neither Miriam St Cloud nor any of the others who had seen my crash would betray me to the police.

CHAPTER 8

The Burial of the Flowers

At last I was about to escape from this suffocating town. I sat impatiently beside Stark as we queued to cross Walton Bridge. It was now late afternoon, and the bridge approaches were filled with traffic returning from London. Although Walton lay to the south of Shepperton, even further from the airport, at least it would spring me from this zone of danger. I was thinking of Stark's decision not to betray me to the police – my apparent return from the dead had temporarily silenced the film actor as it had Dr Miriam, her mother and the fossil-hunting clergyman. Once I left, however, I was certain that Stark would leak the story to a newspaper or television company, particularly when he discovered that I had stolen the Cessna.

But for some reason of his own Stark was deeply impressed by my being a pilot. My spectacular arrival, a real crash as opposed to the contrived mishaps of his film, had tapped some barely formed but powerful dream. He pointed to the almost stationary traffic, the lines of cars stalled in clouds of sunlit exhaust.

'By rights, Blake, you should be a thousand feet above all this. I took some flying lessons once, but I wasn't ready for it. Have you tried hang-gliding?'

I was looking at the dead elms above the park. Around the bend of the river the Cessna's tailplane flicked its message at me. The freshly painted gondolas of the Ferris wheel hung from the sky, toys waiting to be picked up by passing balloonists.

'My real interest is man-powered flight. One day I want to carry out the first world circumnavigation.'

'A man-powered circumnavigation?' Stark rolled his eyes,

eager to humour me. Was he really unaware that he had saved me from the police? 'I'd like to help you, Blake – you could start here in Shepperton.'

'Shepperton?'

'Nowhere better from the publicity point of view. After your crash this morning they'd happily adopt you as their local pilot, you could start a flying school, possibly as a tie-in with the studios. Besides, people around here are obsessed with anything like that – safari parks, dolphinaria, stunt flying, it's all the same to them, they're for ever dressing up as beefeaters or Hanoverian infantry and re-enacting the Battle of Austerlitz. I've decided to build up the zoo. If I could raise your aircraft I'd exhibit it as a show-piece.'

'No ... '

'Why not? Perhaps your insurance company would sell it to me?'

'Leave it where it is!'

'Blake, of course ... ' Surprised by my passion, Stark held my arm to calm me. 'Of course I'll leave it. The river can take it out to the sea. I know how you feel.'

We were now creeping forward across the central span of the bridge. A hundred brake-lights throbbed at my eyes as the drivers stopped and started. An arm's length away, the girders of the bridge moved past, so slowly that I could count the rivets under the flaking paint.

Once again I was sure that we were making no progress. Far from nearing the Walton shore, we were farther away than ever, the lines of cars and buses extending ahead of us like huge conveyor belts. Behind me the Shepperton bank, with its marine contractors and boat-yards, seemed five hundred yards away.

The river swayed. I gasped and lay back in my seat, aware of the vehicles pressing towards me on all sides, moving but immobile, their lights draining my eyes. I waited for the illusion to pass, trapped on this mile-long metal causeway.

'Blake, we're moving! It's all right!'

47

I knew better.

As I opened the door I felt Stark's hand on my bruised chest. Knocking him away with my elbow, I leapt from the hearse. I straddled the waist-high barrier, jumped on to the pedestrian walkway and ran down the slope towards the safety of the Shepperton shore.

Five minutes later, when the river was behind me, I sat down on a bench by the deserted tennis courts. Relieved now of the fear that I had carried across the bridge, I massaged my bruised chest. At least I knew that Stark had not tried to revive me – the hands that marked my ribs were larger, the size and strength of my own.

I looked up at the dead elms, and at the distant streets and houses. For some reason known only to the interior of my head I was trapped in this riverside town, around which my mind had drawn a strict perimeter, bounded on the north by the motorway, on the west and south by the winding course of the Thames. I watched the traffic moving eastwards to London, certain now that if I tried to leave by this last door of the horizon the same queasy perspectives would unravel in front of me.

Two teenage girls and their mother approached the courts, rackets in hand. They eyed me warily, puzzled by the sight of this young priest in his tennis shoes, no doubt drunk on the communion wine. I was tempted to spend the afternoon playing tennis with these women. For all my exhaustion, I was gripped by the same powerful but indiscriminate sexual urge that I had felt for all the people I had met in Shepperton since my crash, for Stark, for the blind child and the young doctor, even for the priest. In a hot reverie I stared at the mother and her daughters, as if they were naked, not in my eyes, but in their own. I wanted to lure them with the promise of a confessional conducted between the baseline returns, mate with each of them among the cross-court volleys, mount them as they crouched at the net.

Why had I trapped myself in Shepperton? Perhaps I was still thinking of the passenger in the aircraft, some mechanic I had overpowered when I seized the Cessna, and unconsciously was refusing to leave until I freed his body. Had this unknown passenger tried to kill me in a last desperate convulsion? I seemed to remember us wrestling together in the submerged cockpit of the Cessna, his hands crushing the air from my chest, mouth clamped on mine as he sucked the last breath from me to keep himself alive for a few final seconds . . .

The women had stopped playing. Balls in hand, they watched me silently, mannequins in a dream. From the scuffed earth at my feet, the dust rising into the air, I realized that I had been mimicking this titanic underwater combat, wrestling with myself in front of these women.

Unnerved by their strange gaze, I shouted some obscenity at them and set off across the park.

The sun, which all day had hung directly over the river like a forgotten spotlight, now lay above the film studios to the north-west of Shepperton. The foliage in the park was more sombre, and the light below the trees seemed to be trapped for a few last hours, unable to replenish itself. Somewhere nearby, in a small meadow beside the park hidden from me by a dark wall of rhododendrons, the three children played together. David's heavy feet thudded through the grass, Jamie hooted away, blind Rachel issued her brisk little instructions.

Remembering this likeable trio, I decided to join them in their game. I pushed through the rhododendrons into the meadow, a narrow tract of forgotten ground that ran down to the river beside a small stream. I watched the children playing in the deep grass. In their make-believe world they walked in single file towards a flower-bed freshly dug in a secret arbour among the trees. The good-humoured mongol was in the lead, followed by Rachel and Jamie carrying bouquets of faded tulips.

They stood solemnly beside the flower-bed. Rachel knelt down, searched the broken earth with her quick hands and laid the tulips among the display of daisies and buttercups. I saw then that the flower-bed was a grave, and that these three handicapped children were holding a funeral service for the dead tulips they had found in the park-keeper's refuse bins. They had set up a modest crosspiece of sticks and decorated it with bits of coloured glass and silver paper.

Touched by this little rite, I stepped into the arbour. Alarmed, the children turned to face me. Rachel threw the last of the tulips into the grave, her cheeks pinched white as she fumbled for David's hands. Before I could speak they darted off through the long grass, Jamie hooting a bird-alarm.

'Rachel . . . ! I won't hurt you! Jamie . . . !'

Then I saw that they had meant another tenant to share the grave with the dead flowers. The wooden cross had been shaped into the rough image of an aircraft, its wings and tail marked with white crayon.

But was it my Cessna they were burying?

I looked behind me at the secret meadow. The children had vanished. For the first time I sensed a premonition that I might be dead.

Yet from that afternoon, in the deserted arbour, sprang my determination to prove that had I ever been dead, had I drowned in the stolen aircraft, I would now for ever be alive.

CHAPTER 9

The River Barrier

'Am I dead?'

I spoke quietly into the grave, waiting for it to reply. Angrily I stared at the aircraft on its cross, and at the suffocating rhododendrons.

'Am I dead and mad?'

Why was I so affected by this infantile game played by three handicapped children? I kicked the flowers from the grave, pushed through the dusty foliage and stepped back into the park. Immediately the light trapped below the trees rushed towards me, happy to find something living to seize upon. It played cheerfully on the lapels of my suit, flashed and tripped around my white shoes.

I was certain that I had not died. The bruised grass behind my feet, the spent light reflected from the river, the cropping deer and the ragged bark of the dead elms convinced me that everything here was real, and not the invention of a dying man trapped in his submerged aircraft. I knew that I had never lost consciousness. I had climbed from the aircraft before it sank, and remembered standing between the wings as the water swirled around my legs.

I strode towards the river, waving my arms to ward off the light that crowded around me, an over-enthusiastic claque. My premonition of disaster reflected a fear that I had invented everything around me – this town, these trees and houses, even the grass-stains on the heels of Miriam St Cloud – and that I had invented myself.

I was alive now, but at some point had I died? If I had been trapped in the aircraft for eleven minutes, why had no one come to my rescue? This group of intelligent people, a doctor among them, had been frozen in their positions on the

51

river-bank, as if I had switched off their clock-time until I escaped from the Cessna. I remembered lying on the wet grass, my chest crushed by a pair of unknown hands. Had my heart failed briefly, bequeathing to my exhausted brain a presumption of death on which the three children had played with such effect?

I was not dead. I stood on the bank, looking at the calm water and at the untroubled afternoon light. A small dinghy had been pulled on to the beach. I stepped on to the sand and eased the craft into the water. Casting off, I fixed the oars and paddled across the quiet stream.

The cool tide ran with light, masking the black water below the surface. I pressed on upstream, and approached the St Clouds' Tudor mansion. The river drummed against the boat, clicking against the cutwater, computing some urgent total.

I was now in the centre of the Thames. Below me, through the opalescent surface, I saw the white ghost of the Cessna. Quickly I shipped the oars and seized the gunnel. The aircraft rested on the river-bed twenty feet away from me, sitting squarely on its undercarriage as if parked in a submarine hangar. The pilot's door was open, and swung to and fro in the current. I was surprised by the immense span of the aircraft's wings, the outstretched fins of a huge ray.

A shoal of silver fish swarmed around the Cessna, swerving along the wings and fuselage. The reflected light from their speckled bodies lit up the cockpit, for a moment revealing the figure of a drowned man at the controls.

I paddled with one hand, shoulders over the side of the dinghy, my mouth and chin touching the water, ready to drink the acid of my own death. The cockpit was only a dozen feet below me, intermittently lit by the watery sunlight. Wavering shadows crossed the instrument panel and cockpit floor.

Again I saw the dark figure at the controls – my own shadow cast through the water!

Exhausted, I sat among the oars on the floor of the dinghy. In the meadow facing me the cattle cropped peacefully at the deep grass. The bank was only a few oar-strokes away, charmed by the gentle tresses of the water-willows. Here I would go ashore. Now that I had confirmed that I was alone in the aircraft I could leave Shepperton for ever. The walk through this quiet meadow with its contented cattle would revive me before I returned to the airport.

Cooling my hands in the water, I paddled towards the bank. The river busied itself around the dinghy, swarming with thousands of particles, hydra and amoeboid forms, the debris of insects and small plants, minute algae and ciliated creatures. Clouds of waterborne dust swerved through my fingers, on the threshold of life, the animate and the inanimate forming an unbroken spectrum, girding me within their rainbows.

I raised a handful of water to the sun and examined the festering particles. The excited congregation of a miniature cathedral, they crowded the vivid water. I wanted to shrink myself to a mote of dust, plunge into this pool I held in my own cyclopean hands, soar down these runs of light to the places where life itself was born from this colloquy of dust.

Without looking up, I waited for the dinghy to run aground. As the last drops of water fell from my hands I raised my eyes to the opposite shore.

Surrounding me was the immense back of an open river, the silver deck of a sun-filled Mississippi whose banks formed a distant horizon. A thin fringe of trees marked the Shepperton shore, and I could barely make out the half-timbered frontage of the Tudor mansion. Two minute figures stood on the lawn, their faces little more than fading points of light.

Determined to cross the river, whatever illusions might unsettle my mind, I seized the oars and began to pull away strongly. The water surged around the dinghy, and I felt the craft move forwards. Over my shoulder I watched the

Walton shore recede further from me, but I pressed on without pausing. The cuts on my knuckles re-opened, but I was certain that if I continued to row I would break through the perimeter my mind had built around itself. I rallied my spirits, a Columbus urging on his faithless crew, Pizzarro navigating the silent, dreaming Amazon.

My hands slipped on the bloodied oars. I stood up, alone on this universe of water, and drove the dinghy forward with one blade. Both shore-lines had vanished below the horizon. My blood fell from my hands and stained the water. The clots drifted away in long ribbons, pennants celebrating this Homeric journey.

The light had begun to fade. Exhausted, I threw the oar on to the floor of the dinghy. The setting sun had reached the horizon, and the once clear air was now misty and opaque. Faint clouds hovered over the ribboned water, as if strange sea-birds were about to form themselves from the blood and breath of my efforts, chimeras that would feed ravenously on my flesh.

Giving up my attempt to cross the river, I began to row again, setting out on the long journey back to the Shepperton shore. Rushing towards me, the dead elms rose from the bank as if propelled into the air on enormous lifts, the tailplane began its semaphore, the Tudor mansion loomed above the water. With a final swerve, the lawn lurched on to the beach.

I was ten feet from the bank. Miriam St Cloud and her mother stood on the grass in the dusk, the pale lanterns of their faces held together as if to form a beacon for me. As I stepped ashore, stumbling in the wet sand, they came down on to the beach and took my arms. The scent of their bodies lay heavy over the dark flowers.

'Blake, stand still. You can lean against us, we're quite real.'

Miriam wiped my bloodied knuckles. Her face was deliberately without expression, that of a doctor tending a child that has wilfully endangered itself. I could see that she was trying to separate herself from me, seal the door of her emotions in case I involved her in my nightmare.

Mrs St Cloud steered me towards the house. I expected her to abuse me, and I was surprised by her tenderness. All her earlier hostility had gone, and she embraced me with warm arms, holding my head with a firm hand against her shoulder as if comforting her small son.

Had they watched me all evening, paddling desperately by myself only a few feet from where they stood, a child playing his game of Columbus?

'Everything's ready for you, Blake,' she told me. 'We've prepared your room, and we want you to sleep for us now.'

CHAPTER 10

The Evening of the Birds

That evening, as I lay asleep in the master-bedroom of the St Clouds' mansion, the first of what I then thought were dreams came to me.

I was flying across a night sky, above a town which I recognized as Shepperton. Below me was the silver back of the river, its long double bend embracing the boatyards and chandlers by Walton Bridge, the Tudor mansion and the amusement pier with its Ferris wheel. I was following the southerly course I had taken earlier that day in the Cessna. I crossed the film studios, where the antique aircraft sat on the dark grass, and then the raised embankment of the motorway. In the moonlight its concrete surface formed an endless waiting runway. Behind their drawn curtains the inhabitants of this small town lay asleep.

Their dreaming minds sustained me in my flight.

As I passed above their heads I knew that I was flying, not as a pilot in an aircraft, but as a condor, bird of good omen. I was no longer asleep in the bedroom of the St Clouds' mansion. Although aware of my human mind, and exhilarated like no bird by the plunging air and the spear-like branches of the dead elms, I realized that I now had the visible form of a bird. I sailed grandly through the cold air. I could see my huge wings and the fluted rows of ice-white feathers, and feel the powerful muscles across my chest. I raked the sky with the claws of a great raptor. A coarse plumage encased me, reeking with an acrid odour that was not the scent of a mammal. I tasted the foul spoor-lines that stained the night air. I was no graceful aerial being, but a condor of violent energy, my

56

cloaca encrusted with excrement and semen. I was ready to mate with the wind.

My cries crossed the rushing air. I circled the Tudor mansion. Hovering by the windows of my bedroom I saw my empty bed, the sheets flung back as if some deranged creature had struggled with ungainly wings to free itself. I swerved across the lawn and chased my moonlit shadow among the flower-beds, touched the water with my talons and sent two plumes of vivid spray above the drowned Cessna.

Eager for the sleeping townspeople to join me, I flew over the silent houses, crying to the windows. On the tiled roof of the hairdressing salon a white form huddled. One wing feebly touched the air, as this lyre-bird struggled free from the sleeping mind of the middle-aged spinster lying in her bedroom below. I circled above her, urging this sensitive creature to trust the air. Across the London road, above the butcher's shop, two falcons clambered along the sloping tiles. The male tested his wings, free spirit of the genial tradesman who lay asleep in the deep double bed above a night store hung with sides of beef and pork. Already his wife had broken free. She strutted across the roof, testing her eager beak on the scents of the night air.

Encouraging them to follow me, I flew up and down the moonlit street, crying softly to these first companions I had raised from their sleep. Timorously the lyre-bird extended her wings and leapt into the night. She fell towards the garden below, about to impale herself on a television aerial, then seized the air and climbed up to join me. But I was not yet ready to mate with her on the wind.

All over Shepperton birds were appearing on the rooftops, raised by my cries from the sleeping minds of the people below, husbands and wives wearing their brilliant new night plumage, parents with their excited nestlings, ready to mount the air together. As I soared above them I could hear their eager cries and feel the beat of their wings overtaking mine. A dense spiral of flying forms rose into the night, an ascending carousel of wakening sleepers. Pairs of whooper swans rose from the apartments above the supermarket, secretary birds lifted from the bungalows by the film studios, golden eagles from the grand houses by the river, a flock of waxwings and house-sparrows from the tents of a sleeping scout-troop beside the motorway.

Followed by this concourse of birds, I flew across the park to the river. The night air was white with thousands of flying creatures. Together we circled the mansion. Miriam St Cloud lay asleep in her bedroom, unaware of the eager suitors I had brought with me. Crying to her, I soared to and fro above the dark garden, hoping to rouse her from her dream.

I wanted us all to mate with her on the wind.

Around me the night air was filled with buffeting and screaming birds. The huge flock was filled with lust, driven frantic by this dreaming young woman. I felt their beaks and talons scramble at my wings as they tried to merge themselves with my plumage, share with me Miriam St Cloud's sleeping body. Their wings beat the air away from me, suffocating me in a vacuum of feathers.

Losing my grip on the sky, I fell towards the amusement pier, fighting my way free from this tornado of screaming birds. Exhausted, I reached the spire of the church and alighted on the roof. As I furled my wings, I was aware of the immense weight of my body, and of the great feathered arms that crushed my chest and drew me back towards sleep.

Beneath my claws the lead panels gave way. Unable to spread my wings, I fell backwards into the dark space below, and struck the tiled floor of a small room.

I lay exhausted between my ungainly wings, surrounded by tables on which the partly dismembered skeletons of strange creatures were displayed. Beside a microscope on an inclined desk I saw what seemed to be the skeleton of a winged man. His long arms reached out as if to seize me and bear me away to the necropolis of the wind.

CHAPTER 11

Mrs St Cloud

I woke to feel a mouth press gently against my lips, a hand caress my chest. River light flooded the room, pouring through the high windows that faced the bed. The morning sun had crossed the water-meadow and glared down at me as if it had been trying to wake me since dawn.

When I sat up Mrs St Cloud was watching me calmly from the window. She stood where I had first seen her after the Cessna's crash, one arm raised to the brocade curtains, but all her nervousness had gone and she seemed more like the capable older sister of her daughter. Had she kissed me while I slept?

'Did you sleep, Blake? You've brought us some unusual weather. There was an extraordinary storm last night – we've all been dreaming of birds.'

'I woke once . . . ' Remembering my night-dream and its exhausting climax, I was surprised by how refreshed I felt. 'I heard nothing.'

'Good. We wanted you to rest.' She sat on the bed and touched my shoulder, gazing at me in a maternal way. 'It was exciting, though, some sort of electrical storm, we could hear thousands of birds rushing through the air. There's been a fair amount of damage. But I imagine, Blake, that all the strange weather you need is inside your head.'

I noticed that she had let a small but glamorous wave into her hair, as if she were expecting a lover. I was thinking of my dream, the vision of night-flying with its nightmare ending, when I had been suffocated within a vacuum of beating wings and fallen through the roof of the church into a strange room of bones. The authenticity of the vision unnerved me. I could remember my swerves and plunges

60

through the air over the moonlit town as vividly as the flight of the Cessna from London Airport. The crying of the lust-crazed birds, my own weeping for Miriam St Cloud, the wild power of the plummeting bodies, the cloacal violence of these primitive creatures together seemed more real than this civilized and sun-filled room.

I raised my injured hands, which Dr Miriam had bandaged before I slept. The ragged lint, and the chafed skin of my forearms and elbows was pitted with small black particles, as if I had been grappling with a flint-covered pillow. I vaguely remembered running from the church in the moonlight. The harsh smell of the birds, the coarse beauty of the air hung about my body, the acrid odour of sea-birds feeding on still-living flesh. I was surprised that Mrs St Cloud had not noticed the odour.

She sat beside me, stroking my shoulder. Wary of her, I lay back against the pillow, surveying the bedroom into which the mother and daughter had carried me after my futile attempt to cross the river. What made me uneasy was that they had both been expecting me, as if I had lived in this house for years as one of the family and had just returned from a boating accident.

How could they have been certain that I would return? The two women had undressed me with an uncanny sense of physical intimacy, as if they were unveiling a treasure they were about to share. I watched Mrs St Cloud move around the bed, take my suit from the wardrobe and brush the lapels as if concerned for the pressures of my skin on the fabric, the traces of my body left on this hand-me-down serge. I felt my bruised ribs and mouth – both still as tender as they had been the previous afternoon – and thought of my dream. It had been no more than the sleeping fantasy of a fallen aviator, but my power over the birds, the way in which I had conjured them from the darkened rooftops, gave me a sudden sense of authority. After the years of failure, of never finding a life that fitted my secret notion of myself, I had briefly touched

61

the edge of some kind of fulfilment. I had flown as a condor, the superior of the birds. I remembered my sexual authority over them all, and wished that Miriam St Cloud had seen me as this greatest of the raptors. Then I would have enticed her into the sky, as some shy albatross. But for that sudden panic of aerial lust, and the collapsing roof of the church, I would have mated with her on the deep bed of the night air.

Thinking of my fall, I asked Mrs St Cloud: 'Is there a museum here? With a collection of bones?'

She laid the priest's suit across the bed, smiling as she stroked the fabric. 'Why, Blake – are you going to leave yours to it? As a matter of fact, there is, in the vestry of the church. Father Wingate's a keen palaeontologist. The Thames here apparently produces the most unusual specimens. Pre-historic creatures, fossil fish – ' she pushed my hair from my forehead ' – not to mention marooned pilots.'

'The vestry roof – was it damaged in the storm?'

'Yes, sadly.' She leaned through the window and waved to someone on the lawn below. 'The police are here.'

I leapt from the bed and stood naked behind her. Two uniformed policemen were crossing the lawn with Dr Miriam. As the three handicapped children played around the sergeant, he pointed to the cattle feeding in the meadow across the river. Obviously he knew that the Cessna had flown across the park on its way south from London Airport, but was unaware that the aircraft lay in the water no more than fifty feet from him. Its white ghost hovered below the sunlit surface.

'Blake . . . ' Mrs St Cloud tried to calm me. 'They won't bother you.'

Confused, I was trying to decide whether to run for it, or bluff my way past the police. Miriam had stepped on to the narrow beach and stood there in her white coat, as if shielding the aircraft from the policemen while she made up her mind about me. The children followed her, squealing with forced excitement at the water, these threatening waves around

62

their feet. They ran with outstretched arms, Rachel a small blind aircraft in formation between Jamie and David. Jamie rooted his leg-irons in the wet sand and squinted at the sky, hooting to the rhythm of the Cessna's tailplane as it switched to and fro in the branches of the dead elm.

Mrs St Cloud caressed my shoulders, but I was looking at her daughter. Hands deep in her pockets, she gazed up at the window, shrewdly weighing my future in her steady eyes. She had released her hair from its tight bun, and this captive fleece now played freely around her shoulders, testing the river air like the eager birds I had seen in my dream. What beautiful and barbarous creature would she have become, some chimeric being to shock the morning air?

'They're going.' Mrs St Cloud waved to the sergeant. 'Heaven knows why they were here.'

I watched the policemen salute and walk back to their car. Mrs St Cloud was looking at the bruises on my chest. As she fondled my body, her eyes raiding my skin, I knew she was unaware of taking part in the unconscious conspiracy to guard me. The witnesses of my crash had constituted themselves as a protective family. Stark was my ambitious older brother, Miriam my bride. But if Mrs St Cloud had cast herself in the role of my mother, why was she so openly attracted to my sex? I remembered the tolerant way in which Miriam had watched her mother undress me the previous evening, well aware of her aroused sexuality.

Taking advantage of her, I pressed her hands to the bruises on my ribs. Her slim fingers barely spanned the blue profiles.

'Mrs St Cloud – while I lay on the beach you were standing here. Did you see anyone revive me?'

She stroked my shoulder blades as if feeling for the stumps of my wings. 'No, I don't think anyone dared to. Blake, I was too frightened to think. You were in the water for so long. I know I attacked you – I was angry with you for being alive, when I'd already accepted that you were dead.'

'I'm not dead!' Angered, I pushed her away. 'I ought to leave!'

'No . . . You can't leave now. Miriam says she'll find you a job at the clinic.'

She lowered her eyes to the floor as I placed my arms around her waist. I steered her from the window, like a naked mesmerist with a middle-aged woman in trance. After I undressed her we lay together on the bed. She hid her face against my chest, but I knew that she could smell my acrid odour, the tang of condor's sebum which the strong sunlight brought from my skin. As I embraced her, placing my bruised mouth on her lips, I was proud of this harsh odour. She tried to push me back, gagging on the stench, her eyes fixed on my bruised skin. Kneeling across her, and placing her legs around my waist, I remembered the huge wings that had carried me above the night sky. I imagined myself and Mrs St Cloud copulating on the air. I knew that there were four of us present, locked in a sexual act that transcended our species – she and I, the great condor, and the man or woman who had revived me and whose mouth and hands I could still feel in my skin.

'Blake . . . you're not dead!'

Mrs St Cloud seized my hips. Her gasping mouth was smeared with blood milked from my lips. I wrestled with this middle-aged woman, pressing her broad shoulders into the pillow, my bloody mouth around her lips and nostrils, and sucked the air from her throat. No longer concerned with her sex, I was trying to fuse our bodies, merge our hearts and lungs, our spleens and kidneys into a single creature. I knew then that I would stay in this small town until I had mated with everyone there – the women, men and children, their dogs and cats, the cage-birds in their front parlours, the cattle in the water-meadow, the deer in the park, the flies in this bedroom – and fused us together into a new being.

Mrs St Cloud struggled, knees kicking at my thighs. With my arms around her chest I crushed her lungs. Unable to breathe, she fell back. Feebly, her heels struck at my calves. As we sank together my mind cleared into a dream of birds, the four of us fusing on the wing . . .

Beside me Mrs St Cloud lay exhausted, lungs pumping the sunlit air through her bloodied mouth. She lay on her back, a shaking hand searching for mine, her freckled legs stretched out as if they were dead. Dark bruises were coming through the raw skin of her breasts and stomach.

I waited beside her, aware that I had nearly killed this woman, who had been saved only by my self-suffocation. Sitting up, she touched my chest, feeling for my diaphragm as if to make sure that I had begun to breathe again. As she dressed she stood beside the bed with her bloodied mouth and chest. She looked down at me without hostility, well aware of what she had done.

I realized that she took for granted that I had tried to kill her, this mother who had given birth to a violent and barbarous infant, wrestling me from her body.

Before she left she paused by the window. Almost absent-mindedly, she said: 'There's a vulture on the lawn. Two of them. Look, Blake – white vultures.'

CHAPTER 12

'Did You Dream Last Night?'

Vultures – ! As I ran down the staircase, buttoning the priest's jacket around my chest, I guessed that the carrion birds had escaped from Stark's zoo, attracted by the odours released from the corpse still trapped in the Cessna. I stood on the terrace by the conservatory, expecting to see the white vultures dismembering the passenger's body. The lawn glistened like chopped glass. A fierce storm had disturbed the night. Pools of water lay in the sunlight among the gravel paths. Along the Shepperton shoreline the leaves of the plane trees and silver birch had been washed of all dust. By contrast, the water-meadow on the opposite bank seemed yellow and faded.

'Pelicans . . . ' Relieved, I watched the two ungainly birds waddle across the lawn. Presumably the storm had brought them inland, though the open sea was fifty miles away. They dipped their heavy bills among the gladioli, uncertain what they were doing in the grounds of this Tudor mansion, among these ornamental trees and flowerbeds.

On the beach below me was a more sinister arrival. A large fulmar was gutting a pike, its talons tearing apart the bloodied flesh. With its beaked bill and strong body, this arctic predator resembled nothing that flew over the placid valley of the Thames.

I picked a stone from the pathway and hurled it at the beach. The fulmar took off down river, lazily trailing the pike's viscera. The damp sand carried its reflection, slick with the fish's blood running into the water.

I stepped on to the beach, which was littered with driftwood and hundreds of coarse feathers. A canvas bag filled with Father Wingate's archaeological tools still lay on the sand, beside a fresh crevice in the pebble bank exposed by the splash-wave of the plunging Cessna. Some six feet long and ten inches deep, this stony shelf was wide enough to take a man. I was tempted to see if it would fit me, and imagined myself lying in it, like Arthur at Avalon or some messiah sleeping for ever in his riverine tomb.

Ten feet from me the sand glittered with silver light, a dissolving mirror leaking into the river. A gondola of the Ferris wheel lay in the shallow water among the Edwardian pillars. Dislodged by the night's storm, a section of Stark's amusement pier had collapsed into the river, carrying part of the merry-go-round with it. A small winged horse lay among the debris on the wet beach.

I remembered my dream, and the bodies of the frantic birds colliding above the fairground as they scrambled around me in the whirling air. Soon after dawn the river had disgorged this antique Pegasus on to the same beach where I had swum ashore. I approached the horse and pulled it on to the bank. The fresh paint silvered my hands, leaving a speckled trail across the sand.

As I wiped the paint on to the grass, the pelicans watched me from the flowerbeds. The same vivid light flared from their plumage. The foliage of the willows and ornamental firs seemed to have been retouched by a psychedelic gardener with a taste for garish colours. A magpie swooped across the overlit lawn, feathers brilliant as a macaw's.

Stimulated by this display of light, I stared into the stained water. The storm had disturbed the river, and a congregation of eels swarmed in the shallows. Heavy-bodied fish moved about in the deeper water, as if they had made their home in the drowned fuselage of the Cessna. I thought of Mrs St Cloud and our strange and violent sex together, and of the birth we had mimicked of an adult child. Already, responding to the nervous irritation of this Sunday morning light, I felt a new surge of sexual potency.

As I left the St Clouds' garden and entered the park I

passed a fallow deer rubbing its muzzle against a silver birch. Only half-playfully, I tried to seize its hind-quarters, feeling the same sexual attack towards this timid creature that I felt even for the trees and the soil underfoot. I wanted to celebrate the light that covered the still drowsing town, spill my semen over the polite fences and bijou gardens, burst into the bedrooms where these account executives and insurance brokers lazed over their Sunday papers and copulate at the foot of their beds with their night-sweet wives and daughters.

But was I still trapped in Shepperton?

For the next hour, while the streets were deserted, I carried out a complete circuit of the town. Following the line of the motorway, where my first escape attempt had been baulked, I set off towards London, where the open fields gave way to a series of quiet lakes and water-filled gravel pits linked by causeways of sand. Leaving behind the last of the houses on the east of Shepperton, I climbed through a hedge and walked across a field of poppies to the nearest of the lakes.

An abandoned gravel conveyor and the rusting shells of two cars lay in the shallow pools. As I approached them, the air swayed around me. Ignoring this, I pressed on. Suddenly the perspectives of lakes and causeways inverted warningly. The muddy ground swerved around me, and then fled away on all sides, while a distant cluster of nettles on a concrete outcrop rushed towards me, gathering around my legs as if to embrace me.

Without a second thought I there and then gave up all attempts to escape from Shepperton. My mind was still not ready to take its leave of this nondescript suburb.

However, if I was trapped here, I at least would assign myself absolute freedom to do whatever I chose.

Calm now, I crossed the field and returned to the town. As I re-entered the quiet streets the first residents were cleaning their cars and trimming their hedges. A party of freshly scrubbed children was setting off for their Sunday School. They walked past the overbright gardens, unaware that I was following them, caged satyr in tennis sneakers ready to seize their little bodies. At the same time I felt a strange tenderness for them, as if I had known them all my life. They and their parents were also prisoners of this town. I wished that they could learn to fly, steal light aircraft . . .

A kite rose from a garden near the film studios, a paper and bamboo rectangle on which a child had painted a bird's head, the beaky profile of a condor. Following its path across the skyline, I noticed a mansard roof I had seen in my dream. There were the same stepped faces on which a pair of ospreys had slithered, the dormer window with its decorated lintel.

Beyond the perimeter fence of the film studios the antique aircraft were drawn up on the grass by the canvas hangars. There were Spads and Fokker triplanes, a huge stringed biplane of the interwar years, and several wooden mock-ups of Spitfires. None of them had been here when I first flew over Shepperton, but I had seen them on the night grass during my dream.

Looking around me, I realized that I had also seen these houses before. The lower floors were unfamiliar, but each of the roofs and chimneys, the television aerials I had nearly impaled myself upon, I recognized clearly. A man in his fifties with his teenage daughter emerged from an apartment house, watching me warily as if unsure whether I was about to beg from them. I remembered the striped canvas awning of the topmost balcony, the pair of mating hawks I had urged into the night sky.

I was certain that the daughter recognized me. When I waved to her she stared at me in an almost fixated way. Her father stepped into the road, warning me off.

Trying to calm them, I raised my bandaged hands and blood-stained knuckles.

'Tell me – did you dream last night? Did you dream of flying?'

The father shouldered me aside and held tightly to his daughter's arm. On their way to church, they had obviously not expected my messianic presence outside their front door. As they hurried away my nostrils caught beneath the heavy scent of cologne the acrid but familiar odour that still clung to their freshly bathed bodies.

Two middle-aged couples passed me with their adult children. I strolled along with them, to their irritation sniffing at them from the gutter.

'What about you – did any of you dream of flying?'

I smiled at them, excusing my shabby parson's suit and white shoes, but I could smell the same tangy odour, the stench of aviaries.

I followed them into the town, trailing their aerial spoor. A dozen large sea-birds circled above the shopping centre, a species of deep-water gull that the storm had brought up the river. On the roof of the supermarket a raven perched, two golden orioles clambered over the ornamental fountain by the post office. On all sides a confused avian life had materialized on this quiet Sunday morning above the heads of these church-going people. Attracted by their acrid scent, duped into recognizing the townsfolk as members of their own species, the birds swirled into the shopping mall. The heavy gulls stumbled across the decorative tiles, wings flurried among the polished shoes. An embarrassed woman laughed nervously at a gull trying to alight on her hat, a stiff-backed old man in brown tweed shook his shooting stick at a raven eager to perch on his shoulder. Children ran laughing among the orioles that leapt from their hands, plumage flaming among the television sets and washing machines in the appliance-store windows.

Badgered by the birds, we moved through the centre of the town, past the overbright foliage in the park, to the church by the open-air swimming-pool. Here at last the birds lifted away, as if repelled by the immense numbers of feathers that lay on the roofs of the cars parked by the churchyard, torn loose during some dizzying aerial tournament.

To everyone's surprise, the church was closed, its doors chained and padlocked. Puzzled, the parishioners stood among the gravestones, prayer-books in hand. The old man raised his stick to the clock tower. Several of the Roman numerals had fallen from the dial, and the hands had stopped at a few minutes past two o'clock. The flagstones around the church were covered with feathers, as if some huge pillow had burst upon the spire.

'Are you the curate?' A young wife I had followed from the town centre gathered enough courage together to point to my suit. I could see she was unable to reconcile its clerical cut with my muddied tennis shoes and blood-stained hands. 'The service should begin at eleven. What have you done with Father Wingate?'

As her husband drew her away the old man in the tweed suit stepped forward and touched my shoulder with the handle of his shooting stick. He peered at me with the gaze of the retired soldier still suspicious of all civilians. 'Aren't you the pilot? You came down in the river yesterday. What are you doing here?'

The parishioners gathered around me, a frustrated congregation. My presence on the ground unsettled them. They would have preferred me safely in the air. Could they sense radiating from my mind those inverted perspectives which had trapped me in this small town?

Raising my bandaged fists, I stepped through them to the doors of the church, lifted the heavy knocker and struck three times. I was irritated by these timid people in their well-pressed suits and flowered dresses, with their polite religion. I was tempted to break down the doors and drive them into their pews, pen them there while I performed some kind of obscene act in the aisle – press the blood from my hands against their bleeding Christ, expose myself, urinate

71

in the font, anything to shake them out of their timidity and teach them a fierce and violent dread.

I wanted to scream at them: 'Birds are gathering here in Shepperton, chimeras more marvellous than anything dreamed of in your film studios!'

I pointed to the fulmars circling the church spire. 'The birds! Can you see them?'

While they backed away from me through the gravestones I noticed that an unusual vegetation was springing through the cobbles around the porch, as if from my heels. I was surrounded by a small grove of gladiolus-like plants each some two feet high, with sword-shaped leaves and a trumpet of milk-crimson blossom the colour of blood and semen within its green flute.

I gestured to the parishioners, who stood with their prayer-books and disappointed faces, their embarrassing odour of birds. I was about to urge them to pick the flowers, but they were now looking at the doorway of the vicarage, where Father Wingate stood, quietly smoking a cigarette. He was wearing, not his cassock, but a Panama hat and flowered shirt, the garb of a stockbroker self-consciously starting his vacation. Although his congregation smiled expectantly, waving their prayer-books, he ignored them and locked the door of the vicarage behind him.

Smoking his cigarette, he concentrated his gaze on me. His strong forehead was crossed by a deep frown, as if he had recently received a severe blow to his confidence in the world around him – the news of a close friend's inoperable cancer, perhaps, or the death of a favourite niece. He seemed so preoccupied that I almost believed he had forgotten he was the priest of this parish and was absent-mindedly waiting for me to conduct my own service.

Overhead the gulls had begun to circle again. Led by the fulmars, they surrounded the church, heavy wings brushing the spire, trying to dash the last of the numerals from the clock face and put an end to past time in Shepperton.

Droppings spattered the cars and gravestones. Unsettled, the parishioners backed away toward the swimming-pool.

'Father Wingate!' The retired soldier with the shooting stick called out. 'Do you need our help, Father?' But the priest paid no attention to him. Below the straw hat his strong face had shrunk into itself. As the gulls shrieked and dived the parishioners scattered among the parked cars.

When the last of them had gone Father Wingate left the vicarage and strode across to the church. Throwing his cigarette among the gravestones, he nodded to me in a matter-of-fact way.

'Fair enough – I thought you'd come.' He stared at my clerical suit, almost hoping not to recognize me. 'You're Blake, the pilot who landed here yesterday? I remember your hands.'

CHAPTER 13

The Wrestling Match

Despite this welcome, the priest made no effort to be friendly. The strain of physical aggression I had noticed after my rescue the previous day was still present. As we approached the church he forced me to walk behind him. I sensed that Father Wingate would have liked to wrestle me to the ground among the lurid flowers springing from my heels. He kicked the blossoms out of his way, lunging at them like a bad-tempered goal-keeper. As I tried to avoid him my feet slipped in the rain-soaked feathers.

Father Wingate held my shoulders. He stared at my bruised mouth, aligning me against some set of specifications in his mind.

'Blake, you look dazed. Perhaps you haven't yet come down to earth.'

'The storm kept me awake.' I pushed his hands away from me. Under the floral shirt he was sweating heavily. Unlike his parishioners he did not smell of the birds. But then nor had I seen him in my dream.

Testing him, I asked: 'Did you see the birds?'

He nodded sagely to himself, acknowledging that I had scored a point. 'As it happens, I did.' He gestured towards the clock tower with his Panama hat. 'There were some strange ones aloft last night. According to my housekeeper the whole of Shepperton slept with an aviary inside its head.'

'Then you saw the same dream?'

Father Wingate unlocked the doors of the church. 'So it was a *dream* . . . ? I'm relieved to hear you say so, Blake.' He stepped through the doors and beckoned me to follow him. 'Right – we'll get this over with.'

As I peered into the nave through the warm, musty air Father Wingate tossed his straw hat on to the font. He turned in the dim light, as if about to attack me. When I stepped back he lifted one end of the nearest pew. He dragged the oak form across the aisle, scattering the hymn books across the tiled floor.

'Blake, take the other end. Let's put our backs into it.'

I lifted the pew, able to see little more than the priest's floral shirt in the thin light. I could hear him breathing hoarsely, like an animal in its burrow working up to some private crisis. Together we carried the heavy seat to the west wall of the nave, then returned for the next pew. Father Wingate moved with the impatient energy of a scene-shifter given five minutes to clear the church. Had he rented the building to the film company for some scene in their aviation spectacular? He tossed the worn velvet cushions out of his way, shouldered the lectern to the vestry door, stacked a dozen prayer-books on to his left arm and tipped them into a tea-crate behind the font. At any moment I expected a studio pantechnicon to drive up with a contingent of set designers and actors in flying gear, ready to transform this parish church into a Flanders aid station, a front-line chapel gutted by the forces of darkness.

Father Wingate returned from the vestry with two dust-sheets and closed the doors of the organ loft. He pulled the candles from the silver sticks, and draped the altar and crucifix with a white sheet.

'Blake, are you still here? Don't stand there dreaming about your birds. Roll back the carpets.'

As we moved around the murky nave, dismantling the interior of his church, I watched the priest at work. Sweat filled the deep seams of his face, and fell in bright drops to the scuffed tiles under our feet. During a brief break he sat with arms and legs outstretched along one of the pews. A large man, I decided, in the grip of some small obsession, using me as a short cut to deal with his own problems. He looked up at the stained-glass windows, as if calculating how to pull them down on to the floor of the nave.

For all his energy, did he understand what he was doing? Had he too seen that premonitory vision of the holocaust? It occurred to me that he was responding in the most sensible way, packing off everything that could be moved to safe-keeping, clearing the pews to one side so that the nave could be used as a refuge, a real first-aid station against that death from the sky.

But his brusque handling of the prayer-books and hymnals, of the gilt-framed portraits of saints and apostles which he heaped into the wooden crate, convinced me that he had some other motive, some scheme in which I was to play a role. Father Wingate was clearing the decks of his life with too much relish.

Without thinking, I found myself rising to his physical challenge. We moved from pew to pew, dragging these lengths of spent timber against the walls. I pulled off my jacket, exposing the bruises on my chest. As we struggled with the heavy forms I knew that I was wrestling with this fifty-year-old priest, matching my wrists and shoulders against his. Separated by the length of each pew, we jockeyed for position on the damp tiles, straining at the huge stiff snake we held between us.

Carried away by the sweat that smeared the stone floor, and by the smell of our bodies, I happily watched the blood spring from my knuckles. An almost homo-erotic excitement had seized me. I dragged the last of the pews across the open nave, twisting it out of the priest's hands as he tried to keep up with me. Like a son showing off his strength and stamina, I wanted him to admire me.

'Good, Blake . . . I'm exhausted. Good.'

Breathing harshly, Father Wingate leaned against his thighs in the centre of the dust-filled nave. Flecks of my blood stained his floral shirt. He was still unsure who I was and what had brought me to Shepperton, but he looked up at me with the sudden affection of a man who has wrestled with a stranger he discovers to be his own son. From that moment I felt a complete trust in this renegade priest.

Later, when I had swept the floor of the nave, Father Wingate unlocked the doors and let the fresh morning air clear the dust from the church. He watched the wind stir the sheets draped over the altar and font, flick the pages of the discarded hymn books. Unimpressed by this act of self-vandalism, he calmly replaced the straw hat on his head. He slipped an arm around my shoulders to support himself, and let me lead the way to the vestry.

His hands did not fit the bruises on my chest. Once again I felt a surge of warmth for him, a regret that he had not brought me back to life. Never before had I known a sense of dependency upon a man older than myself, a pride in his confidence in me. Now I was the returning prodigal, the young flying priest, not only his son fallen from the sky but his successor.

Already the elements of strange ceremonies and bizarre rituals were taking shape in my mind.

Father Wingate opened the vestry door. Immediately I saw the bright sunlight that shone through the large hole in the roof, illuminating the broken tiles on the floor and the specimen cases that filled the room. Behind their glass panels lay shards and knobs of worn bone, all that was left of some ancient fossil beach.

'Before I leave I'll have the roof repaired for you.' Father Wingate knelt among the tiles and picked up a bloodied feather. 'A huge bird fell through here during the storm. One of the condors must have escaped from Stark's zoo – he's careless with those creatures of his.'

I took the feather from him and raised it to my mouth, tasting again the smell of the night air, the sebum of my wings. Father Wingate led me to the laboratory table, equipped with a microscope and lens stand. In my vision I had seen the complete skeleton of a winged creature, but mounted below the lens was a single splinter of bone the shape of a small trowel, its gnarled profiles and pitted seams exposed by the light. Barely a bone, it was so old that it had begun to revert to its mineral origins, a node of calcified time memorializing a brief interval of life millions of years earlier.

Father Wingate placed me over the lens, in which the bone swam like an ancient planet.

'I found this on the beach within seconds of your arrival, Blake. The wave from your aircraft must have dislodged it, in a way you're its co-discoverer. It's certainly my most remarkable find yet. I'm guilty of keeping it to myself. But for a few days ... Anyway, let me introduce one aviator to another. This will have to be confirmed, of course, but I'm almost sure that it's part of the fore-limb of a primitive flying fish – you can see the point of attachment for its wing membrane. A true flying fish, a precursor even of archaeopteryx, the most ancient known bird.'

He stared at his treasure, a hand reassuringly on my arm as if aware of the link between my own nearly fatal flight and the long journey which this winged forbear of mine had taken through geological time to reach our rendezvous on this specimen table. Sunlight fell through the roof, touching this bone, the relic of a new aerial sainthood.

'Father Wingate, tell me – why are you leaving?'

The priest stared at me, surprised that I should need to ask. He placed his large hands on the display cases. 'Blake, this is now my real work – even if you'd not come I would have had to give all my time to it. By the way, I shouldn't have tired you out. I know the next few days are going to test you.'

I looked up at the ragged hole in the roof through which I had fallen in my dream. I turned to Father Wingate, suddenly needing to describe my strange vision, my fears of having died and the way in which I had marooned myself in Shepperton.

'The crash, Father, you were there. Dr Miriam says I was under the water for at least ten minutes. For some reason I feel that I'm still trapped in the aircraft.'

'You're not, Blake! You freed yourself!' He held my shoulders tightly, almost trying to provoke me to stand up for myself. 'Blake, it's why I've closed the church. How it happened, I don't know. But I do know that you survived. In fact I almost believe that it was not death you survived but life. You survived *life* ... '

'I didn't die.'

'Believe me, Blake, since yesterday I've felt that it's not you who are alive but we here who are dead. Seize every chance you have, however strange.'

I thought of the car-park outside the clinic, and my near-rape of Rachel.

'Yesterday, Father, I tried to rape that blind girl – why, I don't know.'

'I saw you – but you stopped yourself. For all we know, vices in this world may well be metaphors for virtues in the next. Perhaps you can take us all through that doorway, Blake. I've felt the same demented impulses ... '

He was staring through the lens at the fragment of his winged fish. I took the bottle of communion wine from the brass table behind him, deciding to get away from this church. I had made this sympathetic but confused priest into my father, another member of the family I had constituted around myself from the witnesses of my crash. I had seen these fossils before. Each of the bones I remembered clearly, etched by the moonlight as I lay on the floor among these specimen cases, listening to the screaming of the birds as they struck in their sexual frenzy at the church tower. I remembered the shin bones of the archaic boar, and the barely human skull of a primitive valley dweller who had lived by this river a hundred thousand years earlier, the

79

breast bone of an antelope and the crystalline spine of a fish – together the elements of a strange chimera. I remembered too the terrifying skeleton of the winged man.

On an easel by the laboratory table, its fine paper marked by splashes of water, was the drawing on which Father Wingate had been working when I crashed. He had completed the sketch as the aircraft sank, his reconstruction of this winged creature, which I too had become as I swam ashore, part man, part fish and part bird.

CHAPTER 14

The Strangled Starling

Vivid blossoms swarmed among the graves, their semen-gorged petals feasting on the sun. Drunk on the communion wine, I set off across the park, the half-empty bottle in one hand. Beyond the deserted tennis courts lay the river, an over-excited mirror waiting to play a trick on me. Everywhere the air had become a vibrant yellow drum. A heavy sunlight freighted the foliage of the trees. Each leaf was a shutter about to swing back and reveal a miniature sun, one window in the immense advent calendar of nature.

I could see the same intense light in the eyes of the deer that followed me towards the clinic, in the mercurous bark of the silver birch, in the inert trunks of the dead elms. But for the first time I felt no fear. My meeting with Father Wingate had made me understand what it was like to feel a father's confidence, part of the same assurance I had drawn from Mrs St Cloud. Both of them I had touched with my blood. It was this sure heart's ground under my feet, my fixed place at last in time and space, that gave the air its vibrancy.

Already I was convinced that the light came as much from me as from the sun.

Calming myself, I reached the empty car-park of the clinic. A few old people sat on the terrace of the geriatric unit, watching with interest as I emerged bottle in hand from the trees. The clinic had shut for the day. I had hoped to see Dr Miriam, partly to tell her of Father Wingate's closure of the church – her waiting-room would be fuller than usual the next day with mourning parishioners in a psychosomatic swoon – but also to show off to her my new confidence.

Bottle to my lips, I stared at the signposts outside the

clinic, with their lists of diseases like destinations. I waved the bottle encouragingly at the elderly patients. By coupling with them, with the fallow deer in the park, with the magpies and starlings, I could release the light waiting behind the shutter of reality each of them bore before him like a shield. By annealing my body to theirs, by fusing myself to the trunks of the silver birches and dead elms, I would raise their tissues to the fever-point of their true radiance.

The bottle shattered at my feet, spilling the last of the wine across my tennis shoes. Blearily I gazed round for something to do, someone I could bother with my messianic delusions. Beyond the clinic the children were playing in their private meadow, moving in their timeless dream through the overlit grass. David's broad head drifted among the poppies, square balloon bearing the image of his amiable face. Behind him came Rachel, smiling serenely as she raced through the blood-tipped flowers. Jamie whooped along with his pivoting stride, face raised to the sun as if seeing his expression in its mirror.

Delighted to be with them, I left the car-park and stumbled towards the meadow. The children animated the deep grass with their secret games. Recognizing me, they let out hoots of delight. They swerved around me, squealing as I blundered after them with my arms raised like an aircraft's wings. I saw a white flag flash between Jamie's legs.

'I'm behind you, Rachel ... ! Jamie, I'm flying over you ... !'

I lunged through the grass after them, aware that I was not really playing. If I caught one of these children ...

Luckily they slipped past me, trailing the white flag like a snare, and disappeared through the arbour towards the river.

I entered this shady bower and approached the grave, this ambiguous memorial to the flowers. I could see how hard the three children had worked, and just how much my arrival had inspired them. Dead daisies and poppies filled the grave, and the wooden cross was decorated by a strip of white metal, part of the wing-tip of the Cessna torn away by the current and washed ashore.

Intoxicated by the scent of the dead flowers, I decided to rest in this luxurious grave. The sun was now overhead, and the warmth trapped within this secluded meadow had agitated thousands of insects. Cicadas chittered and screeched, dragonflies leaked electric glimmers on to the stifling air. On a branch of a silver birch ten feet from me sat an unusual visitor to this riverside town, a scarlet macaw whose resplendent plumage barely held its own in the spectrum of excited light. The meadow lay engorged upon itself, swollen by every sap-filled leaf.

Grandly, I lay back among the flowers. As the sun warmed my bruised chest I felt the surge of sexual energy that had pursued me all day. I thought of Dr Miriam and her mother, and of the three children. I needed to couple with them, with the swaying elders and the warm ground, rid myself like a golden snake of my glowing skin. Again I was sure that this abundant life had sprung from my own body, broadcast from my pores and from the hand-shaped bruises around my ribs.

Two fallow deer had entered the meadow and were muzzling the warm grass. In my mind I entered the bodies of these timid creatures. I dreamed of repopulating Shepperton, seeding in the wombs of its unsuspecting housewives a retinue of extravagant beings, winged infants and chimerized sons and daughters, plumed with the red and yellow feathers of macaws. Antlered like the deer, and scaled with the silver skins of rainbow trout, their mysterious bodies would ripple in the windows of the supermarket and appliance stores.

Searching for the communion wine, I rooted among the flowers. My hand came up with a feathery purse, hidden here by the children. I remembered that Dr Miriam had given me no money for my return fare to the airport. About to open the purse, I found myself holding the still warm body of a strangled starling. I stared at its speckled feathers and limp neck, listening to Jamie's exaggerated hooting beyond the trees. Irritated by the sunlight, my skin had broken out in an attack of hives. Weals like the stings of invisible hornets rose on my arms and chest, as if another creature was trying to share my skin.

I needed to shed this skin.

I clambered from the grave, brushing aside the cloud of petals that fell from my shoulders, and ran through the grass towards the river. Birds rose on all sides, hundreds of starlings and finches, the fleeing residents of a demented aviary. People were flocking to the park, attracted by this bright Sunday morning, summer doubling itself in the brilliant flowers. Young couples lay together on the grass. A father and his son flew a huge box kite. A troupe of amateur actors in Shakespearian costume rehearsed on the green, and the local arts society was setting up an open-air show, the modest paintings drowned by the raucous shrieking of a macaw.

Suffocating in the overheated sunlight, I ran down to the river. I knocked over a small girl tottering after a white dove. Setting her on her feet, I placed the bird in her hands, and sprinted past the tennis courts. The balls flicked at me on the ends of whips, stinging my eyes. Hoping to see Miriam St Cloud, I ran through the dead elms. A party of sunbathers sitting on the grassy slope cheered me on. I leapt through them, my skin on fire, and dived over a barking dog into the cool water.

CHAPTER 15

I Swim as a Right Whale

I lay in a house of glass, sinking through endless floors of descending water. Above me was an illuminated vault, an inverted gallery of transparent walls suspended from the surface of the river. Carried by the welcoming water, diatoms jewelled the shoals of fish who had come to greet me. I searched for my legs and arms, but they had vanished, transformed into a powerful tail and fins.

I swam as a right whale.

Cooled by the healing stream, this realm free of dust and heat, I propelled myself towards the sun, and broke the surface in a burst of foam. As I hung in the air, showing myself to the hundreds of people on the bank, I heard the startled cries of the children. I lay back and struck the water, driving the sunlight into a frantic maze. Again I leapt at the surface, and hurled the spray from my magnificent shoulders across the delighted children. As I turned in the air the tennis players came through the trees to cheer me on. A fisherman reached into his net and tossed a gudgeon towards me, a silver bullet I caught between my teeth.

As I performed for them, the whole of Shepperton came to watch me. Miriam St Cloud and her mother stood on the lawn of their Tudor mansion, awed by my sleek beauty. Father Wingate unpacked his specimen case on the beach, hoping that my exploding wake would dislodge another rare fossil for him. Stark stood protectively at the end of his amusement pier, nervous that I might shatter its rusting pillars. Urging them to join me, I raced in circles through the surging water, chased my tail for the children, blew spouts of foam through the sunfilled spray, porpoised to and fro across the river in shallow leaps that stitched the air and water into a table-lace of foam.

Below me the drowned Cessna sat upon the river bed on its podium of light. Tempted to escape from it for ever, I swam downstream towards the marina, where the razor-keels of the yachts dipped and cut at my spine. Once I eluded them, I would make my way down the Thames to the open sea, to the polar oceans with their cooling icebergs.

But as I looked back at Shepperton for the last time I was moved by the sight of its entire population standing on the bank. They were all hoping that I would return, the tennis players and Shakespearian actors, the small children and the kite-fliers with their box kite collapsed like an empty gift in their arms, the young lovers and middle-aged couples, Miriam St Cloud and her mother beckoning to me like figures in a dream.

I turned and raced back to them, delighted by their cheers. A young man threw away his shirt and trousers, and plunged head-first into the charged water. Crossed by a dozen bars of light, he broke the surface, transformed into a svelte and handsome swordfish.

Next, a woman in tennis gear slipped down the spray-damp grass and dived into the water. In the rush of bubbles she swerved past me as a graceful sturgeon. Laughing at each other, an elderly woman and her husband let themselves be pushed from the bank by a party of teenagers, then emerged from a cloudburst of foam as a pair of dignified groupers. A dozen children jumped into the rushing water, darted away from me as a shoal of silver minnows.

All along the beach, people were stepping into the water. A father and mother waded through the waves, each holding a child, and were transformed into a family of golden carp. Two teenage girls sat on the beach, their legs in the shallows, delighted by the elegant tails that extended lazily from their submerged waists. Happily they removed their shirts, reclining mermaids with bare breasts. They let themselves be drawn into the water that I swirled gently over them with my huge tail, a lacy quilt tossed across two naked lovers. As their hair dissolved in the foam they became two playful dolphins, and slipped away through the water crowded with scrambling pikelets and minnows. An overweight woman in a flowered dress collapsed breathlessly in the water and surged away as a stately manatee. The troupe of Shakespearian actors stepped self-consciously into the unsettled stream, the women raising their crinolines from the sand-stained foam, then sank through the surface, transformed into the players of an underwater pageant, a school of angel fish ruffed with translucent gills and plumed with delicate tendrils.

A few people still hesitated on the bank. I leapt through the crowded waves, urging them to leave the suffocating air. The party of tennis players threw aside their rackets and dived into the water, whipped away as handsome white sharks. The butcher and his attractive wife tottered down the grassy slope, immersed themselves and sailed off as immense sea-turtles with rolling carapaces.

Almost all Shepperton had joined me in this new realm. I cruised along the bank, past the discarded kite and tennis rackets, the still playing radios and forgotten picnic hampers. Only one group remained, watching me from their familiar positions, Miriam St Cloud and her mother, Father Wingate on the beach, Stark and the three children. But their faces were without expression, veiled by the spray as if in a deep dream from which I was excluded.

At that moment I knew that they were not yet ready to join me, and that it was they who were the sleepers.

Leaving them, I drifted downwards into the sunlit water. Led by the swordfish, a huge congregation surrounded me, shoals of porpoise and salmon, groupers and rainbow trout, dolphins and manatees. Drawing the sun's rays with me, I sank towards the river bed. Together we would lift the aircraft and carry it downstream to the estuary of the Thames and the open sea, a coronation coach in which I would lead the inhabitants of this small town to the great deeps of their real lives.

The sunlight faded. A few inches from me, through the water-dimmed windshield, a once-human face grimaced at me. A drowned man wearing an aviator's helmet, his mouth fixed in a death-gape, lay across the controls, arms swaying towards me in the current that flowed through the cabin door.

Terrified by this wavering embrace, I turned and swam blindly into the tail of the aircraft. The air rushed from my lungs in the violent water. No longer a whale, I struck out for the surface through the hundreds of scattering fish. Torn from the aircraft, a fragment of white fabric sailed upwards through the water. Following it, I fought my way to the surface. In a last exhausted race for the sun I seized the air.

I woke in the insect-filled meadow, lying on the wet flowers that filled the grave. A few steps away the three handicapped children watched me from among the poppies. I was drenched in the sweat that soaked my jacket and trousers, and too tired to speak to them. A strange headache was leaving me. I breathed unevenly, as if for the first time, and tried to focus my eyes on the vivid birds and flowers within the meadow. I was aware again of my bruised mouth and chest, as if the dead occupant of the aircraft I had glimpsed in my dream had tried to drown me.

But for all the reality of the meadow, I knew that this warm grass, these dragon-flies and poppies belonged to another dream, and that my fever-vision of swimming as a right whale had been another window into my real life.

I rose to my feet and brushed the petals from my suit. The children moved away through the grass, subdued by whatever they had seen. The strangled starling lay among the dead daisies. Jamie turned on his shackles, avoiding my eyes, but his small face was puckered with concern, as if he wanted to guide me through the ordeal of my vision. In his hands he held a dead sparrow, another purse to be hidden in the grave.

When they had gone I walked alone through the late afternoon, my damp suit covered with a coat of rainbows, a confetti of petals, celebrating my marriage with the meadow.

People were leaving the river on their way home, the tennis players and young parents with their children, the old women and their husbands. Their faces were lit by an energy I had never seen before. As they passed me I noticed that all their clothes were damp, as if they had been caught in a sudden shower.

CHAPTER 16

A Special Hunger

It was now, after this second vision, that I and Miriam St Cloud first began to understand what was taking place in Shepperton. When I left the park and approached the Tudor mansion Miriam was waiting for me on the lawn. She watched me walk towards her across the spray-soaked grass, shaking her head at this irresponsible patient wilfully putting his health at risk. I knew that she was no longer frightened of me, but still half-hoped that I would leave her once-placid town for ever.

'Blake, can't you get rid of these birds?' She pointed to the screeching sea-birds which circled the foam-flecked water, as if they were players in a discarded fantasy I had left lying around untidily. A flock of petrels and cormorants had joined the fulmars, and a dozen of the heavy-winged predators hungrily raked the river with their beaks, hunting with a kind of plaintive and distracted hysteria for the fish I had conjured from my vision. But those fish now swam in the sun-filled lagoons of my head.

'Blake, do you want me to drive you to the station?' Shielding her eyes from the birds, Miriam blocked my way with her strong body. 'Is there any point in your staying here?'

For all her aggressive stance, she was as angry and concerned for me as a young wife would be. I was sure that in some way she had witnessed my vision, perhaps as no more than a sudden glimpse into that real world which I was slowly unfolding as I drew back the curtains that muffled Shepperton and the rest of this substitute realm. When I took off my drenched jacket her hands ran across my chest and back, searching for any fresh injuries.

'I've been swimming in the river,' I told her. 'You should have come in.'

'The water was lovely, I suppose. You're lucky to be alive – there was a swordfish there.'

'Did you see the whale?'

She shook her head, staring in an almost desperate way at the screaming fulmars. 'Frightening creatures – *you* brought them here, you know. I've had to give Mother a sleeping draught.'

Steering me towards the house, she said calmly: 'Blake, I did see something. Perhaps there was a whale . . . there was some magnificent creature swimming up and down, as if he was trying to come ashore. Lost whales often swim up the Thames.'

She took my arm and helped me across the hall to the staircase, her arms closely around me. As I stripped in the bedroom she folded my clothes with quick hands, like a wife eager to get her husband into bed. Was she already aware of my determination to mate with everyone in Shepperton? I stood naked in front of her, the bruises on my chest and mouth more prominent than ever in the electric light. Smiling in a reassuring way at her unembarrassed stare, I gazed frankly at her body, with its dizzying scents. In my mind I dedicated each of our sexual acts to the crippled children, to the young women and the old, to the trees and birds and fish, to my transformation of this riverside town.

'Miriam, was anyone else in the water with me?'

'A few people – five or six – some of the tennis players. And one of the local butchers, amazingly.'

'No more than that?'

'Blake . . . ' Although I was naked she let me embrace her, pressing her hands against my shoulders. 'We've all been so exhausted – first your crash, and the whole nightmare of your escape. Then the storm last night, the strange birds and all these fish . . . portents of God only knows what. Half the time I don't know whether I'm seeing or dreaming.'

91

'Miriam – am I dead?'

'No!' She slapped my right cheek, then held my face tightly in her hands. 'Blake, you're not dead. I *know* you're not. Poor man, that crash. There are things coming out of your head that frighten me, you're crossing space and time at some kind of angle to the rest of us. Something's happened here, you ought to get away from Shepperton altogether . . . '

My arms steadied her. 'No, I have to stay. There's a lot I want to find out.'

'Then see Father Wingate. I know that's all nonsense, but I can't think of anything else that might help you.'

'Father Wingate handed his church over to me this morning.'

'Why? What does he imagine you're going to do with it?'

'Conduct a marriage ceremony – of a special kind?'

Laughing, she moved my hands from her breasts, as if nervous that I might transform her into a thousand-breasted Diana. 'That's strange. Do you know, Blake, as a schoolgirl I often had a fantasy of being married in an airliner – I think I was in love with a pilot I saw at Orly while changing planes with my parents. For some reason I was terribly keen on the idea of a wedding ceremony held ten miles up in the air.'

'Miriam, I'll rent an aircraft.'

'Again? By the way, Stark's a pilot – of a sort. Like you.'

'But not a real one.'

'Are you, Blake?'

I had recovered my strength after the swim, and could easily have lifted her from the floor on to the bed. But I was thinking of my own dream of flight. Had she really had a childhood fantasy of being married in the air, or had I imposed it upon her? A sickly cyclamen sun touched her hair, the trees in the park, the grass in the water-meadow, my blood itself irrigating all the secret possibilities of our lives. I wanted to mate with Miriam St Cloud on the wing, sail with her along the cool corridors of the sky, swim with her down this small river to the open sea, drown the currents of our love in the ebb and flow of oceanic tides . . .

'Blake – !'

Gasping for breath, she struggled from me. She tore her arms free and struck out at my face with her hard fists. For a moment, as she sucked at the air, she stared at me with real terror. When she ran to the door I felt my bruised mouth, aware that I had begun to crush the life from her lungs as I had done from her mother's.

Later, sitting naked in a high-backed chair by the window, I looked down at the river in the dusk, at the now cerise water through which I had leapt as a right whale, my sleek body dressed in foam like the lace ruffs of the Shakespearian actors. What disturbed me was not my apparent attempt to smother Miriam St Cloud, but that I no longer wished to escape from Shepperton. Already I felt committed to the people here, almost as if I was their pastor. The unseen powers who had saved me from the aircraft had in turn charged me to save these men and women from their lives in this small town and the limits imposed on their spirits by their minds and bodies. In some way my escape from the Cessna, whose drowned wraith I could see in the dark water below the window, had gained me entry to the real world that waited behind the shutter of every flower and feather, every leaf and child. My dreams of flying as a bird among birds, of swimming as a fish among fish, were not dreams but the reality of which this house, this small town and its inhabitants were themselves the consequential dream.

As the night air soothed my bruised chest I sensed the power flowing from my body, filling the river and the park. I was sorry to have frightened Miriam – I wanted her to be the vessel of my transforming lust, and our marriage to be not a rape but a private coronation. I watched a shoal of animalcula swarming in a halo around the Cessna, marine creatures from some warm pelagic deep which had crossed the oceans to swim up the Thames and release their light for me.

As for the corpse in the Cessna, this imaginary body no longer frightened me. I even welcomed its challenge, the duel between us for the domination of this river and town.

All night the people of Shepperton continued to stroll along the river bank. They gazed at the vivid foliage in the park that seemed to glow in the darkness like the forest at the fringes of a tropical city. Father Wingate walked along the beach by the illuminated water, fanning himself with his straw hat. He had recovered from our confrontation in the church and patrolled the shoreline as if to make sure that I was allowed to rest. Once again I felt the presence of my first real family. Together they were encouraging me to fulfil myself and make the most of whatever powers I possessed.

However, when the housekeeper brought me a tray of food I found myself unable to touch the roast meat she had prepared. Although I had eaten nothing for forty-eight hours, I was hungry only for the flesh of my own species. And I would take that flesh, not with my bruised mouth, but with my entire body, with my insatiate skin.

CHAPTER 17
A Pagan God

The next morning, at the start of my third day in Shepperton, I began work at Dr Miriam's clinic. As I set off across the park I reflected that for all her deference to me, and my own messianic delusions, the job was a menial one – I was to clean the corridors and waiting-room, run errands for the nurses. While I dressed I thought of rejecting the job and giving myself more time to explore Shepperton, but Mrs St Cloud's devoted presence, hovering protectively around the untouched breakfast tray, soon unsettled me. She gazed at me in a smiling, but drugged way, as if still affected by the sedative her daughter had given to her the previous evening. In her mind was I her infant son, born to this middle-aged woman from the bed of her dead husband? I was still trying to think of myself as her child, and felt vaguely prudish about our sex together. From the window I watched her talking in the drive to a young delivery man. Her evident interest in him confused me, and I almost felt rejected by her. She was complimenting him on something, her hands touching his shoulders. Clearly I had let an unsuspected dimension into Mrs St Cloud's suburban life.

However, after a night's sleep, and surrounded now by the brilliant day, my confidence returned. I felt flattered by the sunlight that followed me through the trees like a spotlight keeping track of a celebrity. Besides, the clinic was the perfect place in which to lie low while my mind realigned itself – particularly if I was struck by a sudden blackout or brain haemorrhage – and I discovered the real meaning of the events taking place around me. I suspected that a blood-clot deep in my brain might be responsible for my strange visions and for the dislocations of time and space. I felt a keening excitement in the overlit grass and flowers, my mind too close for comfort to the singing filament of a dying light-bulb.

As the sun rose behind me it seemed to overflow from the river, transforming the park and water-meadow into a retinal bayou. Fish of every kind filled the water, schools of roach and pike surged around the drowned Cessna as if glutted on the residue of my dream. I strode through the trees, stretching out my arm to catch the brilliant motes. By the tennis courts I broke into a run, spurred on by the huge increase in illumination. The white marker lines hovered several inches above the clay, as if about to detach themselves from the court and take off across the sky like the aerial matrix of a pilot's head-up display. Catching my breath, I leaned against a jacaranda tree, a strange visitor to this temperate park. The leaves were engorged with illuminated sap, each of the trumpet-shaped flowers a halo of itself. Deer moved through a copse of silver birch, cropping at the electric bark. When I shouted to them their eyes twinkled at me as if the entire herd had been fitted with contact lenses.

The sun was hallucinating, feasting eagerly on the Spanish moss that hung from the boughs of the dead elms. The woody tendrils of liana vines twisted around the sedate chestnut and plane trees. Lilies grew from the forest floor, transforming this formal park into a botanical garden seized and replanted during the night by some crazed horticulturalist.

I leapt across a flower-bed of scarlet tulips overrun by huge ferns and liverworts. A startled macaw clambered into the air beside me. Crossing the park, it shook carapaces of light from its green and yellow wings. Fifty yards ahead of me, Miriam St Cloud walked through the trees towards the clinic, surrounded by a flurry of parakeets and orioles, a young doctor making a house-call on an over-fertile mother nature. Happy to see her, I felt that I had prepared this abundant life especially for her.

'Miriam . . . !' I ran through the parked cars and stopped

96

in front of her, gesturing proudly at the brilliant foliage like a lover presenting a bouquet. 'Miriam, what's happened?'

'It's taken some kind of fertility drug, Blake.' She was throwing berries into a chestnut tree, where a monkey-like creature with a bushy tail clung to a branch, surprised to find itself in this elegant park.

Miriam waved a hand around her head, trying to restrain the overlit air.

'Macaws, parakeets, now a marmoset – what else are you going to bring us, Blake?' She sidled up to me, hands in the pockets of her white coat. 'You're like some kind of pagan god.'

For all her good-humoured banter she looked at me with a certain wariness, thinking of the ambiguous nature of my special talents and not all that eager to face up to them.

'A marmoset?' Recognizing the creature, I jumped into the air, trying to seize its tail. 'It's escaped from Stark's zoo.'

'From the inside of your head, more likely . . . ' Miriam beckoned me towards the clinic. 'You've come to work here – now, what exactly can you do?'

Did she suspect that I was still making love to her mother? She strolled around the grassy verge of the carpark, glancing at her reflection in the polished door-panels and showing off her strong legs and hips to me. What could I do? I wanted to shout: I can fly, Miriam, and I can dream! Dream me, Miriam! Only a few steps behind her, I felt my sex thicken. A pagan god? For some reason I liked the phrase, it reassured me.

Suddenly I was convinced: certainly I was not dead, but as well, I was not merely alive. I was twice alive!

Barely able to restrain myself, I caught Miriam's arm, eager to tell her the good news and embrace her in the back seat of the district midwife's parked saloon.

'Blake, now hold on . . . '

Avoiding my eyes, she pushed me away. I gripped the windshield of her sports car, shaking with sexual violence at myself. As I stared at the ground I noticed that the shoots of some lurid tropical plant were springing through the cracked cement. The blood-milk flowers, like the blossom of an aberrant gladiolus, effloresced between my legs, as if in response to my own sex. I had seen the same flowers outside Father Wingate's church.

All around me the bright flutes poked their blood-tipped spears among the wheels of the parked cars, from my footsteps in the grass verge.

'Blake, they're extraordinary ... Dear, they're beautiful.'

'Miriam – I'll give you any flowers you want!' Rhapsodizing over the thousand scents of her body, I exclaimed: 'I'll grow orchids from your hands, roses from your breasts. You can have magnolias in your hair ... !'

'And in my heart?'

'In your *womb* I'll set a fly-trap!'

'Blake ... Do you always get so excited by everything?' Still unaware of the motive force driving these sexual fuses, Miriam knelt between the cars and began to pluck the flowers. Calm now, I watched proudly as this beautiful young woman carried my sex in her hands towards the clinic. Again I sensed the power that I had felt all day, a power that had poured into me during my last vision. After my dream of flying I had behaved like an injured bird stranded in a small suburban garden, just as I had been trapped in this nondescript town. But after my vision of swimming as a right whale I had been transformed, marking my triumph in having escaped from the drowned aircraft. Now my strength was fed by the invisible power of great oceans that reached up the minute vein of this modest river. I had emerged on to the land reborn, like my amphibian forbears millions of years before me who left the sea to stride across the waiting parklands of the young earth. Like them, I carried memories of those seas in my bloodstream, memories of the deep time.

I had brought with me the majesty of the right whales, the age and wisdom of all cetaceans.

That morning I moved grandly around the clinic with my mop and pail, wheeled the soiled linen to the laundry van, ran errands for the receptionists. I watched contentedly as Miriam carried my blossoms around the surgeries and offices, filling the vases which I collected for her from a cupboard. Among the patients in the waiting-room, the expectant mothers and infertile wives, she set out the vivid flowers of my sex.

Two of the patients were middle-aged women whom I had last seen leaping into the river during my vision of the fish. I remembered them, the local hairdresser and a lawyer's wife, sailing grandly through the crowded water, part of my aquatic congregation. Now they sat among my flowers, concerned only with their varicose veins and menopausal flushes. As I polished the floor around their feet neither of them took her eyes off me.

Later, when the morning clinic had ended, Dr Miriam called me into her office to empty her surgical bin. Pinned to the illuminated screen were the X-ray plates of my head. Miriam stood with her back to the window. A brilliant light filled the park with an almost electric glare, as if one of the location units from the film studios had set up its arc lights.

'The birth-rate here is about to soar, Blake – do you realize that almost every patient this morning was obsessed with the idea of pregnancy? There was even a grandmother asking about a donor insemination.'

She took off her coat and looked at me in a concerned but unamused way. Perhaps she expected me to pull out my penis and get to work? I wanted to reassure her, give her courage to face me and our coming future.

I hovered around her with my refuse pail. The sights and scents of her body flooded my senses. Her clear teeth tapping as she stared at the X-ray plates, her left nostril sniffing at a painted finger-nail, her strong hips on which she rocked from side to side, all these obsessed me. I wanted the franchise on every breath she took, on every thought in her head, I wanted to record her small laughs and absent-minded gazes, I wanted to distil her perspiration into the most jealous perfumes ...

'Have you never had any children, Miriam?'

'Of course I haven't! Though Stark and I –' Aggressively she waved me away, and on a sudden impulse followed me to the door. She held my arm in a sharp grip. 'As a matter of fact, since you arrived I've thought of nothing else. I'm as obsessed as those stupid women ... '

'Miriam, don't you understand ... ?' I tried to embrace her, but she held me off with remarkable strength. 'It's the crash ... you're –'

'Blake, for God's sake ... Last night – you were rehearsing some kind of death. Whether for you or me, I don't want to know.'

'Not death.' For the first time the word failed to frighten me. 'A new kind of life, Miriam.'

When she had gone, setting off on her rounds in the sports car, I stood in her office, and examined the X-ray plates on the display screen, these photographs of my head through which a ceaseless light flowed. It seemed to me that the whole world outside, the trees and the meadow where the children were constructing my grave, the quiet streets with their sedate houses, formed an immense transparent image exposed on the screen of the world, through which the rays of a more searching reality were now pouring in an unbroken fountain.

CHAPTER 18

The Healer

By noon the clinic was empty, except for myself and the receptionist, a volunteer housewife. While I rested in the waiting-room, impatient for Miriam St Cloud to return from her calls, a woman arrived with her ten-year-old son. The boy had broken his arm climbing a tree. The mother complained away neurotically, unsettling the receptionist as she tried to fix a temporary splint.

Unhappy at the child's crying, I went into the surgery to see if I could help, in time to hear the mother remark angrily:

'He's been climbing the banyan tree outside the supermarket. All the children in Shepperton seem to be there. Shouldn't the police do something about it? – it's blocking the traffic.'

The boy was still crying, refusing to look at his reddened forearm with its painful veins. Intending to comfort him, I took his hand. The boy winced, and as he pulled away from me his free fist struck my knuckles. Immediately one of the cuts opened and a drop of blood fell on to his arm, which he smeared frantically across himself.

'Who are you? What are you doing to him?' The mother tried to push me away, but the the boy had stopped crying.

He gave a whoop of delight. Proudly he showed the slim and unblemished arm to his mother, and then darted into the corridor, swinging himself from the door-handles.

The mother stood amazed. Staring at me, she said accusingly: 'You cured him.' Like Dr Miriam, she seemed angry, with the same resentful expression I had seen on the faces of Father Wingate's parishioners.

When she and the child had gone the receptionist gestured me towards Miriam's chair. Her eyes fixed on my scabbed knuckles, moist with their healing tincture of blood, she asked matter-of-factly:

'Mr Blake, are you ready to see the rest of your patients?'

An hour later a large queue had formed inside the clinic. Mothers with their children, an old man in a wheelchair, a telephone linesman with a flash-burn on his face, a young woman with her leg in a bandage, they sat patiently in the waiting-room as I continued to wax and polish the linoleum floors. In some way the news of my miraculous cure had spread throughout Shepperton. Now and then I paused from my work – I wanted the clinic to be spotless for Dr Miriam – and beckoned the next of the patients into the surgery: a teenage girl with acne, an air hostess with menstrual pains, an incontinent cinema commissionaire.

For all of them I put on a show of examining them closely, ignoring their grimaces as I touched them with my blood-flecked hands. In their eyes, clearly, I was some kind of unqualified medicine-man whose reputation had brought them here, where they found themselves appalled by my lack of hygiene.

Even when I had cured them they still looked at me with the same distaste, as if they resented my power over them and refused to come to terms with the impulse that had propelled them here. I soon saw that almost all their ailments were mental in origin – my fall from the sky had clearly fulfilled some profound need which each of them expressed in these sprains and rashes. Most of them were patients on Dr Miriam's house-list. As I waxed the floor around the telephone switchboard I heard her calling in repeatedly to ask the receptionist what had happened to them.

The last of the patients left me, a garage mechanic with an infected throat, his surly voice clearing as he thanked me grudgingly. Behind him, on the steps outside, was the tail of the queue. The three crippled children had come in from their secret meadow and hung about the doors. The boys pressed their noses to the glass panes as I returned to my mop and wax. Whispering a commentary to Rachel, David peered up in a hopefully knowledgeable way at the health service notices on immunization, venereal disease and ante-natal care.

After locking away my mop and bucket, I debated whether to treat them. My talents as a healer I took completely for granted, part of the inheritance bequeathed to me by the unseen powers who had presided over my crash. At the same time I felt almost light-headed about everything, like a groom before his wedding, a burgeoning sense of hunger, lust and power, as if I were about to marry the whole of Shepperton and its people.

The three children waited patiently for me. Despite my affection for them, I feared them. I feared that I might not be able to cure them. I feared the grave they were building for me, and which they might complete sooner than I was ready if I gave them back their powers.

'Jamie, come in. I've got a present for each of you. David, bring Rachel with you.'

Rachel, your eyes.

Jamie, your legs.

David, your brain.

I stood in the doorway, calling them towards me. Strangely, they seemed reluctant now to come to me, nervous of these gifts. As I knelt down, readying three drops of blood on my knuckles, the red sports car drove noisily up to the clinic entrance. Dr Miriam, in high temper, pointed to me from behind the steering wheel.

'Blake – leave them alone!'

She frowned angrily at the brilliant air, trying to shut out the light that poured off the trees and flowers in the park.

Even the floors of the clinic, which I had waxed so lovingly for her, reflected the same glowing air.

Unwilling to confront this beautiful young woman with whom I dreamed of flying, I ran past the crippled children and set off between the parked cars towards the illuminated town.

CHAPTER 19
'See!'

The air was bright with flowers and children. Without realizing it, Shepperton had become a festival town. As I strode past the open-air swimming-pool I could see that the entire population was out in the streets. A noisy holiday spirit rose from thousands of voices. Sunflowers and garish tropical plants with fleshy fruits had sprung up in the well-tended gardens like vulgar but happy invaders of an over-formal resort. Creepers hung from the neon sills above the shop-fronts, trailed lazy blooms among the discount offers and bargain slogans. Extraordinary birds crowded the sky. Macaws and scarlet ibis watched from the roof of the multi-storey car-park, and a trio of flamingos inspected the cars outside the automobile showroom, eager for these burnished vehicles to join the vivid day.

Everywhere a brilliant light spilled across the town, as if from the excited palette of a naive painter of jungles. The open-air swimming-pool was packed with people, diving through the rainbows lifted by the bright spray. I counted a dozen gaudy kites flying over the rooftops, one of them with a six-foot wing-span and the emblem of an aircraft on its white fabric.

Accepting all these compliments to myself, and relieved that Miriam St Cloud had decided not to follow me, I set off towards the town centre. I felt strangely grand, well aware that in some way I had made all this possible. My earlier fears had gone, and nothing that happened here would in the least surprise me. I enjoyed my sense of power over this small town, my knowledge that sooner or later I would mate with all these women in their bright summer dresses strolling and talking around me. I sensed the same impulse, perversely,

105

towards the young men and the children, even to the dogs running along the crowded pavements, but this no longer shocked me. I knew that I had so much to do here, so many changes to make, and that I had barely begun.

Already I was thinking of my next vision, certain now that it would not be a dream at all, but a re-ordering of reality in the service of a greater and more truthful design, where the most bizarre appetites and the most wayward impulses would find their true meaning. I remembered Father Wingate's reassuring comment that vices in this world were metaphors for virtues in the next. But of what strange creatures were these butterflies the metaphors, the smiles on these children's faces, the happy shriek of the small boy I had cured? Perhaps they in their turn masked some sinister truth?

In the centre of the high street, between the supermarket and the filling-station, an enormous banyan tree had appeared. Its broad trunk had split the tarmac, throwing up pieces of torn macadam the size of manhole covers. The wide branches overhung the road and had rooted themselves in the sidewalks. A huge throng of people had gathered around the tree, mothers waving to the high branches, where some thirty children sat among the macaws and parakeets. The tree had blocked all traffic through the centre of the town, and a parked car had been trapped by the rooting branches, already as thick as elephant trunks. The old soldier with the shooting stick stood by his caged vehicle, shouting orders to his elderly wife penned in the rear seat.

As I pushed my way through the crowd it was clear that everyone in Shepperton had declared a local holiday. Even the school had closed. The teachers stood outside the gates, waving to the last of the children who ran screaming towards the banyan tree. Meanwhile the shopkeepers were making the most of this flood of customers. Lines of dishwashers, stereo players and television sets stood in the sun outside the appliance stores, children and birds playing among the cabinets. The manager of the furniture emporium and his assistants were setting out an open-air warehouse of cocktail cabinets, settees and bedroom suites. Exhausted by this jostling bazaar, housewives lay back like thankful tourists on the deep mattresses.

By the entrance to the sweet-shop a group of children were helping themselves to the chocolates and candy-bars laid out on a counter, stuffing their pockets with this undreamt treasure. I waited for the owner to chase them away with his broom, but he lounged good-naturedly in his doorway, throwing peanuts to the macaws.

Across the street was the railway station, where a commuter train was about to leave. The driver waited, head out of his cab, and shouted to the passengers who were still talking to each other on the platform. Secretaries and typists, dark-suited executives carrying their briefcases, they were already hours late on their daily journey to London.

'Blake, you haven't got any ...' A small girl with chocolate-smeared cheeks offered me a handful of sweets. I listened to the hum of the electric engines, tempted to push through the crowd and run for the train. Within minutes I could make my escape forever from Shepperton.

Thanking the child, I walked towards the station. But as I looked out along the steel tracks that ran through the gravel lakes to the east of Shepperton I felt a deep sense of lassitude come over me, a complete loss of concern for the outside world. I wanted to remain here, and explore these talents with which I had been entrusted since my crash. Already I knew that my powers might not extend beyond the boundaries of this small town.

There was an angry shout from the driver. Baffled, he shook his head at these renegade passengers. The empty train pulled away from the station. The passengers wandered along the platform, still talking in a relaxed way to each other. The executives threw their briefcases on to the grassy bank, took off their jackets and loosened their ties. They lit cigarettes for the secretaries and lay back on the warm turf, these once disciplined commuters who should already have spent the morning at their advertising agencies and newspaper offices.

Behind them, a few feet from the abandoned briefcases, a small grove of needle-leaved plants had sprung up against the fence. As I turned my back on the station the first eyes were straying to these cannabis plants and the afternoon day-dreams to come.

Happy to leave them to it, I continued my tour of Shepperton. The town was changing under my eyes. Near the film studios people were out in their gardens. Fathers and sons were hard at work building elaborate kites, as if about to take part in some aerial festival. The once immaculate lawns and flower-beds were overrun with tropical plants. Palmettos, banana trees and glossy rubber plants jostled for a place in the vivid light. Lilies and bizarre fungi covered the grass like marine plants on a drained sea-bed. The air was filled with the racket of unfamiliar birds. Screamers trumpeted from the roof of the supermarket, white storks rattled their bills as they surveyed the town from the proscenium of the filling-station. Around a swimming-pool strutted three emperor penguins, chased by a squealing child.

No one was at work. People had left open their front doors and strolled along the centre of the roads, the men bare-chested in running shorts, the women in their brightest summer gear. Married couples exchanged partners in the most sensible and amiable way, husbands taking the arms of their neighbours' wives and daughters. At one street corner a party of middle-aged spinsters called out teasingly to the passing young men.

Seeing these happy pairings, I thought of the cheerful promiscuity to come. I felt a growing sexual need, not only for the young women brushing against me in the crowded streets, but also for the children who followed me, even for the five-year-olds with their candy-filled hands. Confused by this sinister paedophiliac drive, I was barely aware that I had taken one little girl by the hand, the pretty child with the serious, dark-eyed face who was still trying to give me her supply of free sweets, no doubt concerned by my gaunt expression.

Muttering thickly to her, I decided to take her to the park. I thought of the secret bower and the soft bed of flowers within the grave. Even if the crippled children saw us together – and in a depraved way I wanted them to for their own sake – no one would believe them.

As I steered the child through the crowd, repelled by myself but pulled along by the girl's firm hand, I saw Father Wingate crossing the street towards me. He carried his straw hat in one hand, which he waved from side to side like the flight controller on the deck of a carrier signalling a bad landing. I could see that he knew all too well what was going through my mind. At the same time I felt that he did not altogether disapprove, and in some way had grasped the secret logic of this perverse act.

'Come in here ... ' Trying to avoid Father Wingate, I pulled the child into the doorway of the hairdressing salon. Every chair was filled, the line of assistants working like conjurors at the bizarre headstyles, a splendid confusion of feathers and flared perukes, wings of back-brushed hair, like the plumage of an aviary.

Next door to the salon, the local boutique was thronged with customers, as if every woman in Shepperton had set her heart on a new wardrobe. Racks of wedding dresses stood out on the sidewalk, and in the window the manageress was hoisting a magnificent lace gown over the hips of a plastic mannequin, apparently confident that this was the one garment every woman would select as her first choice. Sure enough, there was a mêlée of customers jostling each other good-humouredly for a view of the wedding dress. There were exaggerated sighs of delight, ironic titters of appreciation as these housewives and secretaries, waitresses and middle-aged executives pulled the gowns from the racks and held them up to each other. They buffeted around me, pressing the gowns to their shoulders and shouting cheerfully at me. I felt that I was in a festival town filled with my brides.

Holding tightly to the crushed hand of the little girl, I remembered the white plumage of the birds clamouring around me, driven mad by lust. The women swayed against me, their voices shriller, creatures of a demented zoo quivering in rut. I shielded my eyes from the overbright sun. A huge macaw with electric blue plumage screeched past my head. Its talons tore methodically at the blood-striped awning. A small boy with the eyes of an insane dwarf whirled a rattle in my face.

Forced against the plate-glass window, I lifted the girl in my arms, tasting her damp, frightened breath in my mouth. I stumbled against a trestle table, and a tray of costume jewellery and wedding tinsel fell to the ground. The women pushed towards me, joined by the crowd packed into the shopping mall, excited visitors on a saint's day surging about for a glimpse of a holy man.

Trying to clear my head, I looked up at the banyan tree that blocked the road. Dozens of children swung from the branches, their figures lit by the glowing foliage as if in some animated stained-glass window. Orioles and parakeets flexed their wings between the children, their lurid plumage leaking across the noisy air.

The hot bodies of the women pressed against my skin, their scent inflaming the bruises on my chest. I felt an uneasy sexual euphoria come over me, the intoxication of some strange hunger. The wedding dresses swayed around me in the heat, swinging together from the hangers the women held before their faces.

Through a gap in the crowd I saw Miriam St Cloud step from her sports car and stare in an almost mesmerized way at the plundered racks of wedding gowns. As I tottered among the women, a bull played by these female matadors

110

each with her wedding cape, Miriam seemed confused and uncertain, the last of my brides who had arrived too late for the ceremony. Did she realize that I had cured her patients so that I could marry them? I knew then that I would soon mate with Miriam St Cloud and with everyone here, with the young men and young women, with the children and the infants in their prams. I might never eat again, but their bodies would feed me their sweat and odour.

Terrified now, the little girl pulled herself from me and ran off through the crowd, chasing her friends among the washing machines and television sets. Almost swooning, I raised my fists against an excited mother who lifted her child to scream into my face. I tripped on the lace train of a wedding gown and fell to the ground at her feet. Exhausted by the noise, I lay there in a happy delirium, knowing that I was about to kicked to death by my brides.

Powerful hands seized my waist and lifted me on to the trestle table. Father Wingate held me in his arms, steadying me against the window. With one foot he swept aside the costume jewellery, and then forced the women back. Under his flowered shirt I could smell the horse-like sweat of his armpits. He watched me with an expression both angry and tender, a father about to strike his son's mouth. I knew that he alone was aware of my resolving destiny, of the immanent future which I was about to enter.

'Blake ... ' His voice seemed to come down from the sky.

I swayed against him. 'Call Dr Miriam. I need ... '

'No. Not now.' He pressed my head to his chest, forcing me to breathe his sweat, determined that I should not retreat from whatever vision he had seen me approaching.

'Blake, take your world,' he whispered harshly. 'Look at it, it's around you here.' He placed his hands on my bruised ribs, pressing his hard fingers into the imprint of those other hands which had first revived me.

'Stand up, Blake. Now, see!'

111

I felt his mouth against my bruised lips, tasted his teeth and the stale tobacco of his spit.

CHAPTER 20
The Brutal Shepherd

A strange glaze came over everything. The crowd had moved back, the women with their children drifting away through the powdery light. Miriam St Cloud still faced me across the street, but she seemed to recede from me, lost in a profound fugue. I was aware of Father Wingate somewhere to my left. He watched me with unwavering eyes, one hand encouraging me forward. Like all the others in the now silent shopping mall, he resembled a sleepwalker about to cross the threshold of the dream.

Leaving them, I set off towards the supermarket and library. There were fewer people on the pavements, ghostly mannequins in the still bright light, one by one slipping away to their luminous gardens. Over everything presided the immense organic fountain of the banyan tree, alone retaining its clear outlines. Around it the whole of Shepperton began to fade. The trees and parkland, the houses behind me, were now blurred images of themselves, the last traces of their tenuous reality evaporating in the warm sun.

Abruptly, the light cleared. I was standing in the middle of the park. Everything stood out with an unprecedented clarity – each flower and petal, each leaf of the chestnut trees seemed to have been fashioned separately to fit the focus of my eyes. The roof-tiles of the houses hundreds of yards away, the mortar of the brickwork, each pane of glass had been jewelled to an absolute clarity.

Nothing moved. The wind had dropped, and the birds had vanished. I was alone in an empty world, a universe created for myself and assigned to my care. I was aware that this was the first real world, a quiet park in a suburb of an empty and still unpopulated universe which I was the first to enter and into which I might lead the inhabitants of that shadow Shepperton I had left behind.

At last I was without fear. I strolled calmly across the park, looking back at the footprints behind me, the first to mark this vivid grass.

I was king of nothing. I took off my clothes and threw them among the flowers.

Behind me, hooves tapped. A fallow deer watched me from among the silver birch. As I moved towards it, happy to greet my first companion, I saw other deer, roe and fallow, young and old, moving through the forest. A herd of these gentle creatures had followed me across the park. Watching them approach me, I knew that they were the third family of that trinity of living beings, the mammals, birds and fish, which together ruled the earth, air and water.

It only remained for me now to meet the creatures of the fire . . .

Antlers sprang from my head, seizing the air through the sutures of my skull. I cropped at the soft pelt of the grass, watching the young females. My herd gathered around me, quietly feeding together. But for the first time a nervous air shivered the leaves and flowers. An almost electric unease hung over the silent park, unsettling the warm sunlight. As I led my herd towards the safety of the deserted town I touched a small female, then mounted her in an anxious spasm. We mated in the dappled light, broke apart and cantered together, the sweat and semen on our flanks mingling as we ran.

Following me, the herd crossed the road and entered the empty streets, hooves tapping among the abandoned cars. I paused at their head, excited by the spoor of unseen predators who might watch me from these silent windows and ornamental gardens, ready to seize my throat and hurl me to the ground. I took another female and mounted her by the war memorial, my semen flicking across the chiselled

114

names of these long-dead clerks and labourers. I moved nervously between the lines of cars. Again and again I coupled with the females, mounting one and then breaking away to take another. Our reflections bucked in the plate-glass windows among the pyramids of cans and appliances, the tableaux of dishwashers and television sets, sinister instruments that threatened my family. My semen splashed the windows of the supermarket, streamed across the sales slogans and price reductions. Calming the females, I led them through the quiet side-streets, coupled with each one and left her cropping contentedly in a secluded garden.

But as I steered them to their places, repopulating this suburban town with my nervous semen, I felt that I was also their slaughterer, and that these quiet gardens were the pens of a huge abattoir where in due course I would cut their throats. I saw myself suddenly not as their guardian but as a brutal shepherd, copulating with his animals as he herded them into their slaughter-pens.

Yet out of that smell of death and semen hanging over the deserted town came the beginnings of a new kind of love. I felt gorged and excited, aware of my powers to command the trees and the wind. The vivid foliage around me, the tropical flowers and their benign fruits, all flowed from my infinitely fertile body.

Thinking of the one female I had not yet mounted, I set off through the quiet streets to the park. I remembered Miriam St Cloud gazing raptly at her wedding gown. As I passed the naked mannequin behind its semen-stained window I could scent Miriam's sweet spoor, leading towards the river and the mansion behind the dead elms. I wanted to show myself off to her, my animal body with its reeking pelt and giant antlers. I would mount her on the lawn below her mother's window, and we would mate in sight of the drowned aircraft.

*

Already the afternoon light had begun to fade, turning the park into a place of uneasy lights and shadows. But I could see Miriam standing on the sloping grass by her house, watching me as I sped through the trees in a series of ever more powerful leaps. I could see her astonishment at my pride and magnificence.

Then, as I approached the dead elms, a figure stepped from the dark bracken and barred my path. For a moment I saw the dead pilot in his ragged flying suit, his skull-like face a crazed lantern. He had come ashore to find me, able to walk no further than these skeletal trees. He blundered through the deep ferns, a gloved hand raised as if asking who had left him in the drowned aircraft.

Appalled, I fled towards the safety of the secret meadow. When I reached the grave I lay down and hid my antlers among the dead flowers.

CHAPTER 21

I Am the Fire

When I woke, a sombre light filled the meadow. Dusk had crossed the park, and the street-lamps of Shepperton shone through the trees. My antlers had gone, my semen-spattered hooves and powerful loins. Incarnated again as myself, I sat in the twilit grave. Around me the secret arbour of the crippled children glowed like an illuminated side-chapel in a forgotten jungle cathedral. I squeezed the sweat from my suit. The fabric was smeared with blood and excrement, as if I had spent the afternoon driving a herd of violent beasts.

I stared down at the grave of flowers, at the hundreds of dead tulips and daisies which the children had gathered. They had added more pieces of the Cessna – another section of the starboard wing-tip, fragments of fabric torn from the fuselage and washed ashore. All too closely, the structure already resembled the original aircraft, reconstituting itself around me.

Through the deep grass the faces of the three children glowed like pensive moons. David's worried eyes gazed out below his huge forehead, still waiting for those absent sections of his brain to catch up with them. Rachel's small features flickered among the dark poppies, a forgotten flame. Now and then Jamie hooted at the air, reminding the sky and the trees that he still existed. They were sad at being excluded from my new world. Had they realized that I could change my form, like a pagan god, into that of any creature I chose? Had they seen me as lord of the deer, strutting at the head of my herd, copulating on the run?

I stood up and waved them away. 'David, take Rachel home. Jamie, it's your time to sleep.'

For their own sake I was concerned that they should not come too close to me.

Leaving them in the dark grass by the grave, I walked through the meadow to the river. The night water seethed with fish – silver-backed eels, pike and golden carp, groupers and small sharks. Phosphorescing animalcula swarmed in dense shoals. I stepped on to the sand, and let the charged water swirl across my tennis shoes, washing away the blood and dung. A huge fish crept into the shallows at my feet. Its eyes watchfully upon me, it devoured the fragments, then withdrew silently into the deep.

White pelicans sat on the roof of the conservatory. The evening air was lit from below by the plumage of thousands of birds, and by the vivid petals of the tropical flowers that had wreathed themselves around the dead elms, together forming an immense corona like the one I had first glimpsed as I climbed from the aircraft.

'I am the fire . . . ' And the earth, air and water. Of these four realms of the real world, three I had already entered. I had stepped through three doors, through the birds, the fish and the mammals. Now it only remained for me to enter the fire. But as what strange creature, born to the flame?

A hurricane lamp flared across the metal railings of the amusement pier, illuminating the thousands of fish in the river. Lamp in hand, Stark jumped from the catwalk on to the pontoon of a steel lighter he had moored against the pier. This ancient craft, which he had floated free from some forgotten creek, was fitted with dredging equipment, winch and crane. Ignoring the heavy-backed fish, the tuna and small sharks that leapt from the water around his ankles, Stark inspected the metal jib and rusty hawsers.

So he still intended to raise the Cessna, and mount it as the prize exhibit in his threadbare circus. He turned his lamp on me, and struck my face with the beam as if gently chiding me for leaving the drowned aircraft unguarded. I could see his canny expression, and that he knew we were engaged in a special kind of duel.

Leaving him, I walked up to the house. The French windows were open to the warm evening, and the lights in the drawing-room shone down over the dust-sheets that covered the settees and tables. The wicker furniture in the conservatory, the long dining-table, the chairs and side-boards had been carefully draped, lamps and telephones disconnected.

Had Miriam and her mother decided to leave, so appalled by the spell I had cast over Shepperton and by my transformation of myself into a beast that they had closed their house and made their escape while I slept in the meadow? Thinking of Miriam, and of her place in the centre of my grand design, I ran up the darkened staircase. My own room was untouched, but Miriam's bedroom had been attacked by a demented housebreaker. Someone had hurled her doctor's coat over the dressing-table mirror, emptied her medical case across the bed and shaken the contents on to the floor. Vials and syringes, a stethoscope and prescription pad lay in the broken glass at my feet.

Macaws fluttered shaggily through the darkness as I left the drive. Beyond the trees by the swimming-pool I could see a faint light swaying through the windows of the church. The stained-glass panelling of the east window had been re-moved, exposing the candle-lit vaulting of the roof.

The vestry door hung open, the display cases with their fossil remains lit by the moon. Although he had abandoned his church to me, Father Wingate had worked hard that day, assembling the primitive flying creature whose ancient bones he had found on the beach. With its out-stretched arms, its slender legs and delicate feet, bones jewelled by time, it more than ever resembled a small winged man – perhaps myself, who had lain these millions of years in the bone-bed of the Thames, sleeping there until it was time to be freed by the falling aircraft. Perhaps the Cessna had been stolen by another pilot, that spectral figure I had seen lost among the dead elms. Had I taken his identity, stepping out on to the beach from my resting-place in the river-bank?

A silver stick of candles burned on the floor of the nave, where only the previous day Father Wingate and I had wrestled the pews against the wall. Behind the cloth-draped altar a ladder rose to the east window, from which all the stained glass had been pulled down and thrown to the floor below.

Mrs St Cloud stood by the altar in her dressing-gown, gesturing uncertainly to the flickering light. Miriam sat calmly on the scuffed floor, one hand moving among the pieces of broken glass. Under the nursing sister's cape I could see the embroidered skirt of a wedding dress which she tried to hide from me, the costume of a novitiate bride. She picked casually at the fragments of stained glass, the sections of ruby halo and disciple's robes, cross and stigmata, the pieces of a vast jigsaw she had already begun to reassemble.

'Blake, can you help me . . . ?' Mrs St Cloud took my arm, her eyes avoiding mine as if they might burn her pupils. 'Father Wingate's gone berserk. Miriam's trying to put all this glass together. She's been sitting here for hours.' She gazed helplessly at the looted church and then turned to her daughter. 'Miriam, come back to the house, dear. People will think you're some kind of mad nun.'

'It's not cold, Mother. I'm perfectly happy.' Miriam looked up from her jigsaw with an easy smile. She seemed calm but deliberately detaching herself from everything around her, preparing herself for whatever violent promise I held out for them all. Yet as she gazed admiringly at my grimy suit I could see that it was only by an effort of will that she suppressed her wish to attack me.

'Miriam, there's the clinic tomorrow . . . there are your patients to look after.' Mrs St Cloud pushed me forward to the circle of broken glass. 'Blake, she's decided to give up the clinic.'

'Mother, I think Blake is more than capable of looking after the patients. He has the hands of a true healer . . . '

I was about to step through the fragments of glass and hold her in my arms, reassure her that I wanted only to take her with me into that real world whose doors I was unlocking. Then I realized that she was sitting there, not merely to reassemble the broken window, but to protect herself from me within this mystic circle, as if I were some vampiric force to be held back by these archaic signs and symbols.

I said to Mrs St Cloud: 'You've closed the house – are you leaving Shepperton?'

Confused, she hid her hands in her dressing-gown. 'Blake, I don't know. For some reason I'm sure that we're all going to leave soon, perhaps within a few days. Do you feel that, Blake? Have you seen the birds? And the strange fish? Nature seems to be . . . Blake?'

She waited for me to speak, but I was looking at her daughter, moved by Miriam's fear of me and by her courage, by her determination to face whatever powers I might hold over her. However, I already knew that when they left Shepperton, Miriam and her mother, Father Wingate, Stark and the three children would do so only with me.

Later, while I rested in my bedroom above the river, I thought of my third vision that afternoon, of my lordship of the deer. Although I had not eaten for three days I felt gorged and pregnant, not by some false womb in my belly, but by a true pregnancy in which every cell of my flesh, every gland and nerve in my brain, every bone and muscle, was swelling with new life. The thousands of fish crowding the dark water, the lantern-like plumage of the birds in the park also seemed gorged, as if we were all taking part in an invisible reproductive orgy. I felt that we had abandoned our genital organs and were merging together, cell to cell, in the body of the night.

I was certain now that my vision that afternoon had not

121

been a dream but another doorway into that realm to which my unseen guardians were guiding me. I had become first a bird, then a fish and a mammal, each a partner in a greater being to be born from my present self. However barbaric I might seem, a minor pagan deity presiding over this suburban town in a shabby suit stained with semen and blood, I felt a powerful sense of discipline and duty. I knew that I should never abuse my powers, but conserve them for those goals which had yet to reveal themselves to me.

Already, like the local spirit of some modest waterfall or doorway, I could change myself from one creature to another. I knew that I had been transformed into a household god, not a cosmic being of infinite power pervading the entire universe, but a minor deity no more than a mile or so in diameter, whose sway extended over no more than this town and its inhabitants, and whose moral authority I had still to define and win. I thought of the corona of destruction I had seen hovering over the roof-tops, and my conviction that I would one day slaughter all these people. I was certain that I had no wish to harm them, but only to lead them to the safety of a higher ground somewhere above Shepperton. These paradoxes, like my frightening urge to copulate with young children and old men, had been placed before me like a series of tests.

Whatever happened, I would be true to my obsessions.

No longer needing to sleep, I sat by the window. Was all sleep no more than an attempt by the infant in its cot, the bird in its nest, by old and young alike, to reach that further shore where I had run with the deer that afternoon? Below me the river flowed towards London and the sea. The hull of the drowned Cessna was lit by the white dolphins that crowded the water, turning the river into a midnight oceanarium filled from my bloodstream. Motes of light flickered from every leaf in the midnight forest, miniature beacons within the dismembered constellations of myself. Looking out at the sleeping town, I vowed to guide its inhabitants to the same happy end, assemble them into the mosaic of their one real being in the same way that Miriam St Cloud put together the pieces of stained glass, transform them into rainbows cast by my body upon every bird and flower.

CHAPTER 22

The Remaking of Shepperton

The next day I began to remake Shepperton in my own image.

Soon after dawn I stood naked on the lawn among the drowsy pelicans. I had roused myself from a deep and undisturbed rest, almost surprised to find the quiet bedroom still around me. The high-backed chair by the window, Mrs St Cloud's desk and dressing-table, the mirror-faced wardrobes against the wall, hung faintly in the dim light as if rejoining me after a long journey. I stepped from the bed on to the carpeted floor, grateful for the soft pile, for the passive air doing as little as it could to unsettle me. I felt like a child in a holiday hotel, senses alert to the smallest blemish in the paintwork of the ceiling, to a strange vase on the mantelpiece, to all the exciting possibilities of the coming day. My skin prickled like over-sensitive camera film, already recording the hints of light that touched the pewter sky above London. Advancing quietly towards Shepperton, the early dawn picked out the mast of a yacht moored in the marina by Walton Bridge, the inclined ramp of a sand-conveyor by the gravel lakes, the lightning conductors on the galvanized roofs of the film studios.

Each of the images left its imprint on my skin, one part of the surrounding world that formed the illuminated fresco of my face and hands. Refreshed by these remote messages, the soft assurances of the day, I decided not to dress for the moment. No one else was awake, and I left the bedroom and made my way down to the hall. Everywhere the draped furniture seemed to be waiting its turn to reconstitute itself.

I let myself through the front door and walked across the

damp grass towards the grey water. The river ran up to me, rubbing itself against the beach as if eager to shed its dark coat. The huge flocks of birds sat quietly in the trees, ready for me to signal them to life.

The first light moved across the water meadow. I stepped on to the beach and raised my arms to the sun. As I stood there naked I knew that I greeted the sun as an equal, a respected plenipotentiary I admitted to my domain. Turning my back to its rising disc, I walked through the cold shallows and admired the hundreds of golden carp that swarmed around my feet.

Followed by the sun, I left the grounds of the mansion and entered the deserted park, an ostler leading a large and passive work-horse out to the day's labour. I ran naked through the trees, pretending to abandon the sun in the topmost branches of the dead elms, but it moved tolerantly through the trees at its steady pace. For the first time since my arrival, I felt confident and free, ready to make the day.

Outside the church I stopped to catch my breath. I remembered Miriam St Cloud on her knees among the stained-glass fragments, playing too calmly with her puzzle. Leaving the sun moored to the church steeple, I entered the vestry, where the ancient bones of the winged man seemed to stir in the morning light.

Naked, I stood below the altar, aware of the faint scent that hung in the air. I could smell Miriam's body around me, her lips and breasts, her nervous hands ready to push me away. Again I wanted to embrace and reassure her. Standing in the glass circle, I held my penis in my hand. I could feel her massaging me as I woke on the wet grass after my crash . . .

Semen jolted into my palm. I stared at the bright fluid and remembered the river water I had held up to the light, a condensed universe of liquid dust.

Leaving the church, I threw the semen on to the cobbled

125

pathway outside the vestry door. As I paused there, looking across the swimming-pool at the replica aircraft in the grounds of the film studios, green-fluted plants with the same milk-red blossoms sprang through the stones at my feet. I stepped among them and set off towards the town, my swollen penis in my hand. As I ran through the trees I thought of Miriam. Again I ejaculated beside the tennis courts, and hurled my semen across the flower-beds.

Immediately a luxurious tropical vegetation uncoiled itself among the staid tulips, breaking the damp soil. The pale leaves of young bamboo shivered against the metal netting. A delicate tapestry of Spanish moss unfurled itself from the branches of a dead elm, a corpse dressed for its own coronation. Strangling vines circled the slim trunks of the silver birch like eager suitors.

Excited by my own sex, I felt light-headed and generous. All sense of hunger had left me. I decided to startle the placid town with my sex, but not by copulating with these suburbanites still asleep in their bedrooms. I would mount the town itself, transform Shepperton into an instant paradise more exotic than all the television travelogues that presided over their lives.

I left the sun to find its own way across the park, stepped on to the deck of the swimming-pool and climbed to the high diving-board. Below me was the resting water, and a tiled floor decorated with tritons and amiable fish, where there were no drowned aeroplanes. The air played on my bruised chest, carrying from the church the scent of Miriam St Cloud.

At the slightest touch, semen spilled into my hand. I let the pearly string fall across the water. Jewelled medallions glimmered on the surface, an electric chemistry rippled to and fro like an invisible swimmer. Within seconds the patterns had coalesced into a series of green saucers each with a white flower at its centre. When I stepped down from the

126

ladder the entire surface of the pool was covered with immense lilies, the playground of a water-cherub.

Leaving the swimming-pool, I set off towards the centre of Shepperton. The great arms of the banyan tree had seized the pavement outside the post office and filling-station, as if trying to pull the whole of Shepperton into the sky. I strode down the empty street, and touched the first of the lamp standards, anointing it with my semen. A fire vine circled the worn concrete and rose to the lamp above my head where it flowered into a trumpet of blossom.

Delighted by this, I marked the road-verge with orchids and sunflowers. Outside the supermarket I set up a line of mangoes in the ornamental urns, their happy fruits breaking through the debris of cigarette packs and fast-food foil. At the filling-station I ejaculated across the fuel pumps, and over the paintwork of the cars standing in front of the showroom. Mile-a-minute vine hung in deep mists over the radiators, gorged itself on the morning air and climbed the glass windows, clutching at the neon signs and roof gutters. Lilies flowered beside the fuel pumps, succulent plants trailed around the hoses, decorating themselves for the first customers.

Already Shepperton was taking on a carnival air, a processional route being prepared for a triumphal motor-cade. I worked rapidly, eager to transform the town before the sleeping residents woke to discover the day. I planted groves of oleanders outside the bank and appliance stores, and threaded flowering vines along the overhead telephone wires, a charming embroidery of the morning's messages. Their nute-shaped flowers formed chains of decorated lights. I stood on the roof of the multi-storey car-park, letting my semen drip on to the decks below. A cascade of cannas and wild strawberries fell from the concrete ledges, turning this grey labyrinth into a cheerful hanging garden.

Everywhere I went, scattering my semen on this dawn circuit of the town, I left new life clambering into the air behind me. Egged on by the rising sun, which had at last caught up with me, I moved in and out of the empty streets, a pagan gardener recruiting the air and the light to stock this reconditioned Eden. Everywhere a dense tropical vegetation overran the immaculate privet hedges and repressed lawns, date palms and tamarinds transformed Shepperton into a jungle suburb.

Already these changes would have been visible to anyone in the surrounding fields, to the drivers on the motorway. When I returned to the car-park soon after six o'clock I could see that I had painted the town with a vivid equatorial palette, an Amazon glaze.

Hundreds of coconut palms were rising from the gardens, the ragged parasols of their leaves swayed above the chimneys. At every street corner groves of bamboo speared through the cracked paving stones. All over Shepperton, from the roofs of the film studios, supermarket and filling-station, the tropical foliage leaked its light into the air. The sun rose over the sleeping town, a slow giant helping me in its ponderous but sure way. Thousands of birds had emerged from the dense vegetation, and kept up a chittering chorus, macaws and cockatoos, gaudy honeyeaters and birds of paradise.

I stood by the entrance to the car-park, listening proudly to this dawn din, and thinking how impressed Miriam would be when she stepped to her window and saw the way in which I had dressed the day for her. Already the first spectators had arrived to admire my handiwork. Two newspaper delivery boys sat on their bicycles under the banyan tree and stared open-mouthed at the brilliant vegetation and at the cranes and scarlet ibis looking down at them from the roof of the supermarket. Seeing me, they stepped back behind their bicycles, too frightened to move. I assumed that they were startled by my naked body and erect penis, by the semen glistening on my thighs, but then I realized that they were unaware of my nakedness, and were awed only by the huge bruises on my chest.

'You two, move along – if you stay there you'll be trapped.' I walked over to them and lifted their bicycles through the roots of the banyan tree. They pedalled away, catcalling as soon as they were out of my reach. Flowers sprang from the handles of their bicycles, orchids threaded themselves through the spokes, they swerved down the empty streets in a flurry of petals.

Outside the bank a postman was waving his arms at the overlit air, trying to drive away a flock of orioles who swooped at the bright stamps in his satchel. As I approached he blundered into me.

'You're up early – did all these flowers wake you?' Too surprised to notice my naked body, he watched me warily as I picked up the bundles of letters. Muttering to himself, he moved off down a quiet side-street. Roses sprang from the envelopes in his hand. Puzzled, he pushed postcards wreathed in vine-leaves through the letter-boxes, tax demands decorated with tiger-lilies, and handed parcels transformed into flowery bouquets to the drowsy housewives.

Last of all, completing my transformation of this suburban town, I walked along the main roads leading to the perimeter of Shepperton. To the south I threw my semen at the foot of Walton Bridge. Standing in the centre of the main road to London, I ignored the hornblasts of the passing drivers. Once again I was sure that none of them realized I was naked, and thought they were looking at an eccentric villager trying to throw himself under their wheels. As I turned my back to them the pale green shoots of bamboo pierced the cracked macadam and quivered fifteen feet in the air, their trunks forming a palisade across the embankment of the bridge, a forest wall behind which the motorists would soon be stranded.

Again, on the road to the airport, at the northern boundary

of Shepperton where only three days earlier I had trapped myself, it was now my turn to seal out the external world. Two middle-aged office cleaners pedalled past me. They laughed good humouredly as I stood in the road, masturbating while the sun waited patiently at my shoulder. When they looked back a grove of saw-bladed palmettos sprang across the road at my feet.

As I returned to the river Shepperton was coming to life, curtains flung back on to the brilliant day and the jungle gardens that crowded the drives and garage roofs. Children in pyjamas leaned from their windows, whooped and shouted at the rainbow clouds of tropical birds. A milkman with a vanload of bottles had parked outside the film studios, and was pointing to the giant ferns and climbing palms that sprawled across the sound stages. Three film actors stepped from a taxi and stared at this transformation as if caught without any rehearsal for a new scene in an Amazon spectacular their demented producer had dreamed up overnight. When I walked past them they stared at my naked body and semen-smeared thighs, obviously assuming that this was the proper costume for their jungle epic.

However pleased I was by these preparations for the day, I knew that all this was only a beginning. I had brought back the primeval forest, but within these tropical vines, behind the lurid plumage of the birds, there waited a harsher world to come. I watched the housewives in their nightdresses lifting bouquets of orchids from their letter-boxes as the postman passed, smiling at these messages from an unknown lover. The whole town was my garland to their night-warm bodies.

But this was only my first day as the presiding deity of Shepperton, as that pagan god of the suburbs Miriam St Cloud had described. I listened to the cawing of great birds, and saw a condor clamber across the roof of the clinic. Its talons seized the tiles like the necks of its prey. It cast a weary

130

eye at me, bored by all this festivity, and waiting for the real time to begin.

Waving away the pregnant deer, I entered the still cool forest. I knelt on the wet grass between the illuminated trees, the once dead elms which were now stirring faintly with life, putting out the first new shoots through the moribund bark. Feeling the sun bathe my naked body, I worshipped myself.

CHAPTER 23

Plans for a Flying School

'Blake, you've prepared a wonderful day for us!' Mrs St Cloud stood at her familiar place by the bedroom window. She pointed to the light that poured from the trees along the Shepperton river-bank, an electric shore. 'It's marvellous – you've turned Shepperton into a film set.'

For an hour I had been lying in the warm morning air, my body cared for by the sun. I was happy to see Mrs St Cloud, as excited as a scout-mistress at some spectacular jamboree. She waited at the foot of the bed, unsure whether she was allowed to penetrate whatever aura surrounded me. She was both pleased and confused, the mother of a precocious child whose talents might veer away in a dozen unexpected directions. I wanted to show off, conjure all sorts of extraordinary treasures out of the air for her. Even though I still had little idea of the real extent of my powers, I could see that Mrs St Cloud took them for granted. That confidence in me was what I most needed. Already I was thinking of extending my domain, even perhaps of challenging the unseen forces who had bequeathed those powers to me.

'Have you seen Miriam this morning?' I was afraid that she might have fled from Shepperton to the safety of London, by hiding in some colleague's chambers while the strange events played themselves out in this small riverside town where her pagan god cavorted among the washing-machines and used cars.

'She's at the clinic. Blake, don't worry, she was upset last night.' Mrs St Cloud spoke of her daughter as some kind of errant wife who had fallen into a silly religious fever. 'She'll understand you soon. I do now – and Father Wingate.'

132

'I know. That's very important.' I waved to the people on the Walton bank who had come across the water-meadow to see for themselves the transformation of Shepperton. 'I've done all this for her. And you.'

'Of course, Blake.' Mrs St Cloud held my shoulders, trying to reassure me. I liked her strong fingers on my skin. Already I had begun to forget that we had lain together on this bed, during my surrogate birth. I was glad that, like everyone else, she had failed to notice my nakedness.

A swordfish leapt from the water, its white sword piercing the air as it saluted me. The river was crowded with fish, an over-stocked oceanarium. Ignoring the dolphins and porpoises, the shoals of huge carp and trout, Father Wingate sat on a canvas chair among his fossil-hunting gear. Hard at work, he sieved away at the wet sand, surrounded by a troupe of curious penguins. The three crippled children were with him on the beach, dragging ashore a section of the Cessna's wing cast into the shallows during the night.

They were all working away as if time would soon run out. It occurred to me that whenever I woke I found the members of my 'Family' in their original places, like so many actors setting up another take in their impersonation of reality. Even Stark, stripped to his swimming trunks, was working on his ramshackle amusement pier. He had loosened the mooring lines of his dredger, ready to float the rusty pontoon above the submerged Cessna. The clumsy jib was entangled in the thick lianas that covered the Ferris wheel. Machete in hand, he slashed morosely at the vines, waving the heavy blade at the watching fulmars.

Unsettled by all this activity, I took Mrs St Cloud's arm. She held me reassuringly to her breast.

'Blake, tell me – what are you going to dream for us today?'

'I don't dream.'

'I know . . . ' She smiled at her clumsiness, pleased by her affection for me. 'It's we who dream, Blake, I know that.

You're showing us how to *wake*.' As a scarlet macaw flew past the window she said, with complete seriousness: 'Blake, why don't you start a flying school? You could teach everyone in Shepperton to fly. If you like, I'll talk to the people at the bank.'

Thinking about this strange but potent suggestion as I stepped on to the lawn, I watched Father Wingate and the three children hard at work on the beach. Why was the renegade priest so keen to discover the remains of the archaic winged creature buried beneath his feet? I smiled at the guilty expressions on the faces of the children, involved in a secret enterprise not in keeping with the spirit of the day. They dragged the section of the Cessna's wing into the undergrowth, so preoccupied that they too failed to notice my naked body.

Teach them all to fly? No one could teach these crippled children to fly, but as for Miriam St Cloud ... Already I visualized us flying together in the sky above Shepperton, escaping for ever from this modest paradise. I left the grounds of the house and let myself through the gates into the park. As I ran past the tennis courts the warm air rushed against my naked skin, eager to lift me from the ground. I needed to find Miriam before she despaired of everything I had done.

On all sides of me parties of people were moving through the trees, children raced among the flower-beds, trying to catch the vivid birds. Drawn to Shepperton by the extra-ordinary vegetation sprouting from every roof-top, by the hundreds of palm-trees lifting their jungle parasols from the suburban gardens, the first visitors were pushing through the bamboo palisades I had set up by Walton Bridge. On the airport road they stepped from their cars and photographed the cactus plants and prickly pear rooting themselves comfortably in the concrete pavement.

A long queue of patients waited for me outside the clinic

134

– old men from the geriatric unit bitten by the marmoset, a woman with a hand she had impaled on a bamboo stake in her garden, two teenage girls who giggled at me nervously, as if certain that I had impregnated them, a young electrician savaged by a nesting osprey on the roof of the post office. They glanced at my naked body without comment, taking for granted that I was clothed. The waiting-room was filled with a platoon of middle-aged women impatiently arguing over the results of their pregnancy tests. My devoted claque, their eyes were fixed on the semen stains that marked my thighs. Had I mounted them all in my vision? Looking at their plump cheeks and pink mouths, I knew that all the tests would prove positive.

'Mr Blake! Please . . . !' The receptionist pushed through the throng of people in the corridor. Exhausted, she clutched at my arm. 'Dr Miriam's left us! She closed her surgery this morning. She seemed strange, I wondered if you . . . '

Taking the keys, I let myself into Miriam's office. I closed the door on the noise outside and stood naked in the darkened room. The hundred scents of Miriam's body, her smallest gestures, hung on the faint light like a caress, a present to me waiting to be opened.

Her desk had been cleared, the drawers emptied, cabinets sealed. Pinned to the wall were the X-ray plates of my head, deformed jewels through which a ghostly light still shone, like that corona of destruction I had first seen over Shepperton. Between them was a holiday postcard from a fellow physician, a reproduction of Leonardo's cartoon of the Virgin seated on the lap of St Anne. I stared at these serpentine figures, with their unfathomable pose. Had Miriam seen my winged form in the bird-like creature, the emblem of my dream flight, that seemed to emerge from the drapery of the mother and her daughter, as I had emerged from Miriam and Mrs St Cloud?

'Mr Blake . . . You'll see your patients now?'

Restlessly, I waved the receptionist away. 'I'm busy – tell them they can cure themselves, if they try.'

I needed to fly.

I pushed through the crowd of women in the corridor and left the clinic. People jostled me, shaking their wounds and bandages, pinning me against the cars. An old woman knelt on the ground at my feet, trying to milk the blood from my knuckles.

'Leave me!' Exhausted by them all, and thinking only of Miriam St Cloud, I grasped the windshield of her sports car, vaulted over the hood and set off towards the church. I tried to think of my next step in the transformation of this town. For all my authority, I still felt the need to prove myself, to explore my abilities to the fullest, even to provoke myself. Was I here to exploit these people, to save or punish them, or perhaps lead them to some sexual utopia . . . ?

I looked up at the vivid tropical vegetation that crowded the rooftops of the town, the hundreds of huge date-palms dipping over the chimneys, the green fountain of the banyan tree. I was eager to get on with the day. I listened to the excited voices of the people outside the clinic, arguing like children among the cars. I wanted them to discover their real powers – if they existed within me, they existed also within themselves. Each of them had the power to conjure a miniature Eden from the ground at his feet.

I wanted to lead them to their true world, across all the tariff lines of restraint and convention. At the same time, on the most practical level, I guessed that I could use the population of Shepperton, not merely as part of my plan to escape from the town and deny finally that death from which I had already once escaped, but to make my challenge against the invisible forces who had given these powers to me. Already I had wrested from them the governorship of this small town. Not only would I be the first to escape from death, but I would be the first to rise above mortality and the

136

state of being a mere man to claim the rightful inheritance of a god.

The church was empty, the milk-red blossoms of my sex choking the porch and the doorway of the vestry, barbarous flowers taller than those disappointed parishioners. Still hunting for Miriam, I ran past the swimming-pool towards the entrance to Stark's amusement pier.

The kiosk had been freshly painted, the desk fitted with a ticket dispenser. When my second coming occurred, Stark would be waiting in his box office. The dredger on its rusty pontoon now floated twenty feet from the pier, its crane cut free from the vines that encircled the Ferris wheel and the merry-go-round.

But why would the people of Shepperton, many of whom worked at London Airport and the film studios, be interested in the shabby wreck of the Cessna? Perhaps Stark guessed that once the news of my extraordinary powers, of my survival of death, reached the world at large the aircraft would take on a talismanic aura that would survive my own departure? Watched by the world's television cameras, people would pay anything to touch the waterlogged wings, gaze into the blanched cockpit from which the young god had appeared ...

I felt the bruises on my chest, almost convinced now that it was Stark who had revived me. He alone was certain that I had died, and that through the narrow aperture of my survival another world was spilling through into this one.

Wings shivered dustily in the darkness below the cages. As its door swung in the air I saw one of the vultures picking in a desolate way at the gravel floor. Its mate huddled against a pile of old packing cases, hiding its shabby plumage from the sun.

So Stark had unlocked the cages of his threadbare zoo and expelled the occupants. The marmoset hung from the outside bars of his cage, locked out of his own home, while the chimpanzee sat dejectedly in a gondola of the Ferris wheel, his gentle hands working the controls as if hoping to fly off to some happier landing ground.

They looked hungry and uncared-for, intimidated by the tropical vegetation erupting around them. I knew they were no part of my renascent Shepperton, but sorry to see them in this neglected condition I knelt down, touched the semen-stains on my thighs and pressed my hands to the ground. When I stood up a small breadfruit tree rose with me, its fruit as high as my head. I fed the marmoset, then walked over to the Ferris wheel and raised a miniature banana tree beside the chimpanzee. He sat in the gondola, head lowered shyly, gracefully unzipping the fresh yellow fruit.

Before I could attend to the vultures I heard Stark's hearse approach, its hoarse engine breathing like a beast. Stark swung the heavy vehicle into the forecourt, throwing the hot dust against my legs. Smoothing his blond hair in a self-conscious way, he gazed at me from behind the wheel, unaware that I was now naked. In his mind he was setting up the first of the television interviews.

As I outstared his insolent eyes, I felt my blood rise. I was tempted to launch a falcon from my arm, a young killer that would seize Stark's throat in its first moment of life. Or a cobra from my penis to spurt its poison into his mouth. But when I walked towards him I saw the struggling plumage of some dishevelled creature in the rear of the hearse. Lying across the steel coffin racks were a dozen birds he had netted. Macaws, orioles and cockatoos, they sprawled helplessly on the floor of the hearse, the new tenants of Stark's zoo.

'They're nervous of you, Blake.' Stark lifted the rear door of the hearse in a grand gesture. 'I trapped this lot in the last half-hour. Shepperton's turning into some kind of mad aviary . . . '

His manner was still wary and ingratiating, as if my increasing power over this small town, my limitless fertility, provoked him to challenge me all the more. I was certain he suspected that these bedraggled creatures snared in the coarse netting were parts of myself.

Careful not to touch me – would I transform him into some sharp-beaked but weak-legged raptor? – he lifted the tail-gate, seized the net and jerked the birds on to the dust at my feet. He stared down at the netted sprawl, at the bruised plumage, obviously tempted to strangle the birds with his bare hands there and then.

'You'll like what I'm doing, Blake. There'll be a permanent record here, one of each species, a kind of memorial to you. Don't you like that, Blake? Already I'm thinking of a dolphinarium, large enough for a whale. But I'll have all the birds here. And in a big cage by the Cessna, there'll be the largest of them all, the king-bird.'

His dreamy eyes roved across my body in an almost erotic fever. 'What do you say, Blake? A condor, for you . . . ?'

CHAPTER 24
The Gift-making

Sitting naked on the war memorial, I decided to enjoy this public holiday. The entire population of Shepperton was already in the streets, celebrating a jubilee. A huge crowd dressed in its summer finery moved around the centre of the town, turning the modest high street into the flower-bedecked rambla of a tropical city. People strolled arm in arm, pointing up to the vines and jewelled moss that hung from the telephone wires, to the hundreds of coconut and date palms. Children swung from the branches of the banyan tree, teenagers climbed into the arbours of orchids and gourds into which the abandoned cars had been transformed. Tapioca plants ran riot in the gardens, overrunning the roses and dahlias.

And the birds were everywhere. The air was a paint-pot of extravagant colours hurled across the sky. Parakeets chittered on every window-sill, rails screeched from the jungle decks of the multi-storey car-park, screamers trumpeted around the fuel pumps in the filling-station.

Looking at them all, I again felt the need to fly.

Beside me a ten-year-old boy clambered up the steps of the war memorial and tried to press a model aircraft into my hands, hoping that I would bless it. Ignoring him I read the names of the dead of two world wars, artisans and bank cashiers, car salesmen and dubbing mixers. I wished that I could raise them from their graves and invite them to the carnival, call them from their resting places on long-forgotten beaches and battlefields. As well, there were those nearer to hand in the cemetery behind the church.

I jumped down from the memorial and moved through the crowd, happy to see them all in such good humour. Outside

140

the railway station the last of the office-workers were once again making a half-hearted attempt to set off for London. But as I approached they gave up all thought of work. Ties loosened, jackets over their shoulders, they strolled through the holiday throng, their sales conferences and committee meetings forgotten.

There was a flurry of activity by the bank. The crowd stepped back, watching quietly as two embarrassed cashiers set up a large trestle-table by the entrance. The younger of the girls shrugged her shoulders in an almost hysterical way as the manageress emerged with a metal cash-box. A tall, refined woman with a scholar's forehead, she opened the box to expose thousands of bank-notes – francs, dollars, pounds sterling, marks and lire – packed together in bundles. As her assembled staff crowded the entrance, watching with fascinated disbelief, she plunged her sensitive hands into the deep notes and began to set out the bundles on the table.

Something blundered into me, a man's excited body, but for the swimming trunks as naked as my own. Stark stepped past me, pushing the people aside. Bird-net forgotten in one hand, he stared at the bank-notes, swaying on his feet like a mesmerized lover.

Able neither to touch the money nor to take his eyes from it, he murmured: 'Blake, dear man, you've got them eating out of your hand . . . '

With a friendly wave to the spectators, beckoning them towards the money she had laid out, the bank manageress returned to her office. No one moved, unable to accept this most mysterious of all gifts. Stark stepped forward, swinging his net like a gladiator. He looked back at me with a wild, conspiratorial eye, obviously assuming that I had contrived all this by some extrordinary sleight of hand. Quickly he loaded a dozen bundles into his net, then turned and strolled off casually through the crowd.

Still undecided, people pressed around the trestle-table. The owner of the television rental bureau picked up a bundle of dollar bills and tossed them to a teenage girl, as if throwing a sweet to a child. In a bravura gesture he took out his wallet and emptied the contents across the table.

All around me people were suddenly giving each other money, tossing coins and cheque-books, credit cards and lottery tickets on to the green baize, happy gamblers betting everything on the certainties of their new life. Beside me a young gypsy with a grubby infant in her arms opened her purse and took out a single pound note. She pushed it shyly into my palm, smuggling a secret message to an unknown lover. Charmed by her, and eager to give her something in return, I rubbed the note between my semen-tacky hands and passed it to her son, who thoughtfully unwrapped it to reveal a tiny humming-bird that hovered in a scarlet blur an inch from his nose.

'Blake . . . here's a million lire.'

'Take all this, Blake – there's more than a thousand dollars. Enough to start your flying school . . . '

Everyone was handing me money and credit cards, clapping delightedly as I gave them back birds and flowers, sparrows and robins, roses and honeysuckle. Happy to amuse them, I spread my arms across the table, touching the wallets and cheque-books, then stepped aside with a flourish. Among the scattered coins a peacock appeared and majestically spread his tail.

In the shopping mall the managers and their assistants were bringing out their goods and giving them away to the passers-by. Again and again I saw Stark, in a heaven of excitement, pushing a loaded supermarket trolley from one store to the next. He had parked his hearse in the side-street by the post office. Shouting to the children to help him, he manhandled two television sets and a deep freezer into the rear of the vehicle, scattered fistfuls of bank-notes from the loaded bird-net.

I let him get on with it, pleased to see him fulfilled. One person at least was needed to show some appreciation of these material objects. Agreeing with me, an amiable crowd followed Stark, urging him on as he loaded the hearse with video-recorders and stereo-players. In a mood of good-humoured irony people gave him money, a man took off his gold wrist-watch and pressed it into Stark's hand, a woman clasped her pearl necklace below his chin.

All over Shepperton a happy exchange of gifts was taking place. Along the once quiet suburban streets, now invaded by the tropical forest, people were setting out tables and kitchen chairs, arranging displays of dish-washers and bottles of Scotch, silver tea-sets and cine-cameras, like so many stalls at a village fête. Several families had moved their entire household effects into the street. They stood by their bedroom suites, rolls of wall-to-wall carpeting, piles of kitchen utensils, like happy emigrants about to abandon this small town and return to the simple life of the encroaching jungle. Laughing housewives gave away their last stocks of food, pressed loaves of bread, jars of relish, fresh steaks and legs of pork through the windows of passing cars and buses.

Amazed by all this generosity, the last of the visitors to Shepperton drove off through the narrowing gaps in the bamboo palisades by Walton Bridge and on the airport road. Loaded with their booty, they looked back at Shepperton like raiders leaving a town that has ransacked itself. Even the nonplussed drivers of two police cars which strayed into the high street left loaded with gifts, the rear seats of their petal-strewn vehicles filled with a burglar's treasure of silverware and cutlery, jewel cases and cash-boxes, the fall-out of this mysterious festival of gift-making.

Watching them proudly, I knew that I wanted to stay with these people for ever.

CHAPTER 25

The Wedding Gown

I was ready to fly again.

It was now noon. The air was still, but a strange wind was blowing into my face. My skin was swept by a secret air, as if every cell in my body was waiting at the end of a miniature runway. The sun hid itself behind my naked body, dazzled by the tropical vegetation that had invaded this modest suburban town. Pausing to rest, the crowd began to settle itself. Mothers and their infants sat on the appliances in the shopping mall, children perched on the branches of the banyan tree, elderly couples relaxed in the rear seats of the abandoned cars. There was a sense of intermission. As I walked across the street to the multi-storey car-park, followed by a troupe of children, I was the only adult still moving about.

And none of them was aware that I was naked.

They were all, I knew, waiting for the next turn in my performance. In their words, they were waiting for me to 'dream' them again. I strolled through these relaxing family groups, who before my arrival would have thought of nothing more adventurous than filming themselves nude in their gardens. I felt proud that they were prepared to entrust all the burgeoning possibilities of their lives to me. Having given away the contents of their larders, they would soon be hungry, a hunger not to be satisfied by the mangoes and breadfruit hanging from the jungle foliage around them. Somehow I was sure that when the time came they would be fed from my flesh, just as I in turn would be fed from theirs.

Surrounded by the children, I climbed to the roof of the car-park and walked across to the concrete ledge. Far away,

144

beyond the park, the swordfish leapt from the river, straining to catch my eye, a signal that I should begin the dream time. All the forces of a benevolent nature seemed to be concentrated on me as I stood here with the sun at my side. The bamboo groves at the foot of Walton Bridge and along the airport and London roads were thicker now, heavy palisades at which the incoming traffic was forced to stop. Passengers climbed from their cars, wary of approaching the cactus and prickly pear. I knew that I had only a little time left to me. Within a few hours Stark would call the television companies, and the camera crews would descend on Shepperton, followed by an army of botanists, social scientists and mental health inspectors.

I felt something pressed into my hand. The small boy who had followed me from the war memorial stood at my elbow, squinting up at me with an encouraging smile.

'Shall I make it fly for you?' When he nodded eagerly I raised the plastic model and launched it into the air. As people ducked, the aircraft swerved between the telephone lines, plunged towards the ground and turned into a darting swallow that swooped across the roof of the post office.

There was a delighted whoop from the children sitting on the roof behind me. Immediately half a dozen model aircraft were pushed into my hands by their clamouring owners. Replicas of world war fighters and bombers, they spun from my fingers when I whirled them across the street, erratic darts that soared away as crested swifts, starlings and wagtails.

While the children ran squealing across the roof only little Jamie was left, standing shyly on his leg-irons with some home-made aircraft hidden in his hands. David was trying to wave him back, his eyes worried under the massive forehead, concerned that this amateur effort would never merit its transformation into a bird.

Did they alone, these crippled children, know that I was naked?

'Jamie, give it to me. I can make anything fly – don't you believe me?'

Had he brought me another dead bird? But as he opened his hands I saw that he held a small fragment of the Cessna's wing, a riveted panel from the section they had dragged on to the beach that morning.

'Jamie!' I tried to cuff his head, angry with this crippled child for playing this macabre game with me, but he darted away on his leg-iron.

From the street below there was a warning shout, then a ripple of giggles from the children in the banyan tree.

'Down here, Blake,' someone called. 'Your first student.'

Walking along the centre of the flower-strewn high street came Miriam St Cloud, dressed in a grotesque but magnificent wedding gown. Pinned together from a hundred yards of white tulle, it resembled a costume worn in some Hollywood spectacular of the 1930s. The huge train stretched behind her, its hem ruffed like the tail-plumage of a bird, carried by little Rachel. Her blind eyes were shut as if dreaming of flight. From Miriam's shoulders the side-panels of the dress formed a pair of immense soft wings waiting to take the air.

Miriam paused in the street below me, a great white bird searching for her sky. At first I thought she was in some kind of religious trance, a profound fugue from which I would never retrieve her. She gazed round at the flowers and vines that covered the supermarket and appliance stores, at the birds on the portico of the filling-station, the timid fallow deer watching her from the blossom-wreathed fuel pumps, as if wondering which of these was to be her groom.

'Dr Miriam, he's on the roof . . . '

'Above you, doctor . . . '

People called to her from the parked cars, pointing to me as I stood out against the sky on the roof of the car-park. But when Miriam looked up at me I could see that she was

146

completely awake, trying in the most sensible way not to be impressed by all this luxuriance, by this hanging garden of orchids and bougainvilia. I was pleased that she admired my powers over the air and the birds, my command of the forest, even though she still suspected that I was some kind of interloper in the proper order of the natural universe.

At the same time I knew that she was at last achieving the secret ambition she had set for herself, this adolescent dream of an aerial wedding. Holding the skirt of the wedding gown in one hand, she walked calmly through the watching crowd, unembarrassed to be seen indulging this pleasant whim in front of her patients.

Yet even then, as she strode firmly towards the entrance of the car-park, I was sure that she was challenging me in her quiet way, and still believed that my powers were limited, infinitely smaller than those of her presiding deity. Was she testing me here, to see if I could teach her to fly?

While she climbed the stairway everyone was silent. From the surrounding streets the last of the townspeople left their houses and came towards us below the jungle canopies. Even Stark was resting from his happy pillage of the town. He sat on the roof of his hearse outside the post office, surrounded by looted appliances and a colourful autumn leaf-fall of bank-notes. He waved to me with a confident smile, certain that whatever I might choose to do next would astonish everyone. I liked him for his complete guilelessness.

At the end of the high street, by the war memorial, Father Wingate was fanning his face with his straw hat. He and Mrs St Cloud had come across the park with the chauffeur and housekeeper, pushing the wheelchairs of three elderly patients from the geriatric unit. They stood together, the priest reassuring Mrs St Cloud that I was in no danger, two provincial parents eclipsed by their son's extraordinary achievements but none the less proud of him.

There was a scuffle behind me. David broke away from the other children and ran up to me. Below his swollen forehead his eyes were unsettled. He knew that he alone had not been let into the secret of the day's happiness. In his hands he held a tattered white rag, a peace offering for Jamie's heartless prank.

'Blake . . . it's for you.'

'David, that's a treasure.'

I recognized a remnant of my flying suit, a ragged section of the left shoulder and waist-band. I pulled it over my head and hips. Dressed in this fragment of my past, I turned to face Miriam St Cloud. She had reached the stairhead and now walked towards me in her wedding gown, ready for her marriage with the air.

Already the wind was moving across the roof of the car-park, lifting the train and wings of Miriam's dress, eager to carry her into the air.

'Blake, can you hold me?'

Steadying herself, she reached for my hands, the shy wife of a gymnastic prodigy unsure what was about to take place but certain that all would be well. I could smell the warm scent of her body, and see the sweat staining the armpits of the wedding dress.

'Blake, you're wearing your flying suit . . . it's in rags.'

'There's enough of it left, Miriam. Now, hold my hands.'

I wanted only to set her free, to fly with her from this town in which we were trapped. I wanted to pass on to her all my powers so that she could escape even if I could not.

I gripped her wrists and led her to the edge of the roof. Seeing the ground five floors below her, Miriam stumbled and released the train. Her hands flurried at the air until they found my shoulders.

The crowd was silent, people sitting under the trees. Even the town's policeman had stopped with his bicycle. Thousands of birds were falling helplessly from the sky, their wings confused by the air that failed to support them. Stranded on the rooftops, they waved feebly to each other.

Macaws and parakeets sprawled in the gutters of the supermarket. Flamingos lay splay-legged on the proscenium of the filling-station. Sparrows and robins plummeted from the still air.

A new kind of sky now covered the town.

I felt an electric fever move below my skin, as I had done during my previous visions, and I knew that once again I was moving through the doorway of my own body into a realm ruled by a different time and space.

'Blake, can we . . . ?'

'Yes, Miriam, we can fly.'

We stood together on the edge of the parapet, our feet over the sill. Miriam held my hands and looked down at the street below, fearful that we would dash ourselves to death among the parked cars. But at the last moment she turned to me with complete confidence, a wish to see me again triumph over the death I had already defied.

'Blake, *fly* . . . !'

I slipped my hand around her waist, and stepped forward with her into the open air.

CHAPTER 26
First Flight

We fell together.

Miriam's hands seized my chest, her nails tearing my skin. Above us there was a cry of alarm, Rachel's blind scream.

I caught our falling bodies and steadied us against the air. In the street below people were running in all directions, mothers tripping over their children. Miriam and I hung together, an arm's length from the fourth floor of the car-park. Through the bougainvilia that spilled over the parapet I could see the cars standing in the shadows on the canted deck. Miriam's white train hung vertically above her, and rose fifty feet into the air to form an immense head-dress.

Calm now, I began to breathe again. A cool air moved up the face of the building and caressed the backs of my thighs, my chest and shoulders. Miriam's eyes still stared at me, drained of all expression as she concentrated on my hands.

I waited for her to breathe. I could feel her skin vibrating, an over-stretched drum. By an effort of will every cell in her body was crossing the threshold into its real domain, reassembling itself particle by particle. At last she grew calm, confident of her mastery of the air. Her hands moved inside mine, feeling for the pulse of my nerves and bloodstream, like those of a novice pilot relaxing her fierce grip. She smiled at me in a tender way, a wife taking part, not in this flight with her young husband, but in her first act of sexual love with him.

The last of the birds fell past us through the air.

Lifting Miriam gently, I propelled us into the sky. We paused above the car-park, waiting as her train settled itself. The sunlight irradiated the panels of her wedding dress,

150

illuminated wings that carried us across the air. The three crippled children squinted up at us from the roof. They clenched and unclenched their small hands, trying to close the distance between our feet and the ground. In the streets below hundreds of people were waving us back, frightened that we would fly too near to the sun.

I looked down at them, recognizing the once familiar townsfolk, now veiled from me as if they were standing on the floor of a glass lake. My true realm was the vivid air, this commonwealth of space and time where we shared ourselves with every photon. Drawing Miriam after me, I climbed higher into the clear sky and took her on a tour of my domain.

Arm in arm, standing in the gondola of an invisible airship, we flew across the rooftops of this jungle town, I in the rags of my flying suit, Miriam in her resplendent wedding gown. Her eyes were open, but she seemed almost to be asleep, staring at me like a happy child excited by a strange dream in which she has glimpsed her first love. Holding her cold hands, I felt that she was now dead, that her body stood in the streets far below me, and that I was flying away with her soul.

We reached the film studios, where the antique biplanes sat on the grass runways. There we turned and followed the trajectory my aircraft had taken when it first approached Shepperton. Far away, the rest of the world, the small towns of the Thames Valley, the winding river and the busy motorways seemed to be veiled by the intense light. We crossed the shopping mall, the supermarket and post office, and flew over the park above the elms to where the Cessna lay drowned beside the beach where I had woken to my second life.

We hovered above the water, Miriam's wedding dress like the spirit of this drowned aircraft. I turned Miriam to face me, overcome by the need to embrace her. She placed her hands on my bruised ribs, even in her sleep trying to ease my

151

pain. As I drew her to my chest a corona of light shivered in the air around us. I pressed her against me and felt her trembling skin. Her face touched mine, her lips forcing themselves against my bruised mouth.

Without pain, our smiles merged into each other. Her cool skin passed through my own, the loom of her nerves ran its quicksilver through mine, the tides of her arteries poured their warmth and affection into the remotest corners of my body. As we embraced she merged with me, her rib-cage dissolved into my own, her arms merged with my arms, her legs and abdomen disappeared into mine. Her vagina clasped my penis. I felt her tongue within my mouth, her teeth bite against my teeth. Our eyes merged, their retinas fused. Our vision blurred, multiple images seen by the faceted eyes of this chimerized being.

Then I saw everything around me with twice my sight, through Miriam's eyes as well as my own. Within our minds I felt her nervous vertigo, her confidence in me and her love for me. Every flower and leaf in the park shone with an even greater brilliance, a forest of illuminated glass created by a master jeweller.

I searched the air, but Miriam had gone, slipping away through the hundred doors of my body. I myself now wore the wedding dress. I felt the weight of its huge train and panels, like the wings of the Cessna. Turning my back to the river, I soared across the park to the centre of Shepperton. There I hung over the roof of the car-park, the wedding dress filling the sunlit air, displaying to the silent people below the chimeric union of Miriam and myself.

As I alighted on the concrete roof David and Jamie ran forward. They held the quivering train of the dress, tethering me to the roof, this strange aircraft that had strayed into the air-space of Shepperton. Standing on the ledge, I let the wings subside and waved reassuringly to the crowd below. Their faces seemed dulled, as if they were unable to grasp what they had seen. Even Father Wingate, fanning himself with his straw hat, seemed stunned by everything, suspended between belief and disbelief. Mrs St Cloud wandered across the road, scanning the air over her head. In some way the sky had mislaid her daughter.

However, I felt stronger for them all now, confident that I was more than merely alive. Miriam's spirit and body had recharged my own. I was tempted to keep her within me, a princess locked in the fierce castle of my soul.

Already I missed her. Aware that there were others I could take into myself, and on whose spirits I could feed, I walked to the centre of the roof. Opening my arms, I released Miriam to the sunlit air.

She stepped backwards from me, taking the wedding dress with her. Her face was blanched by a profound trance, the deep sleep of my body. Seeing her materialize in front of them, Jamie and David ran forward to greet her, Rachel scuttling after them with her blind smile. Together they took her hands. In the street below the retired soldier cheered and waved his shooting stick.

His voice seemed to wake everyone. Rallying themselves, people climbed down from the roofs of the cars, and began talking to each other, aware that the flying display was over.

At the staircase Miriam turned and looked back at me, seeing me for the first time since our flight. As she smiled I knew that she now acknowledged my rule of the air. Her face was still blanched, as if her body had died a little as it made its departure from this small town.

I was certain now that through her, and through the ascending spirits of the people of Shepperton, I could at last make my escape.

CHAPTER 27

The Air is Filled with Children

'Blake, can we fly?'

'Teach us to fly, Blake ... '

Dozens of children surrounded me as I left the car-park. I amiably fended them off, and gazed round with some pride at the flower-decked façades of the stores and supermarkets. After so many exhausting days I now felt transformed, my confidence restored. Not only had I been able to fly again, but I had taken Miriam's body into mine. Like a great bird, I had mated and fed myself on the wing. Could I feed on the people of this town, use their eyes and tongues, their minds and sexes to construct a flying machine that would carry me away? I was almost sure now that my powers were limitless, that I was capable of anything I wished to imagine.

The children tugged and argued with each other while I stood in the shopping mall among the television sets and bedroom suites. A flock of sparrows fluttered around my feet, chasing a scrap of breadfruit. Everywhere the birds were rising into the air again.

'David! Jamie!' I decided to distract them. 'All of you – watch me!'

As the sparrows skittered through the bank-notes I trapped them with my hands, taking them into my palms like a conjuror. They merged quickly with my flesh, and I felt their small hearts flutter within my wrists, a babble of nervous pulses. The children stared open-mouthed, and with a flick of my fingers I released a stunned cock-sparrow. While it straightened its crushed feathers a young falcon perched on a nearby car lunged towards the sparrow. I clapped my hands and absorbed the heavy bird, feeling its

154

resisting talons in my elbows, its powerful wings within my back.

Amazed by these apparent sleights of hand, the children squealed with delight and embarrassment. Jamie hooted at the sky, warning it that I might be capable of anything. Only David seemed uncertain of me. In the doorway of the supermarket he murmured to Rachel, unsure where all this might lead. But for the next hour I strolled around the precinct like a conjuror, applauded by the watching crowd. I drew dozens of birds into my body, snatching them from the air and bundling them through the trap-doors of my hands.

My body was a chittering madhouse of angry birds. I stopped outside the supermarket when David stepped back defensively, muttering a warning to Rachel. While the children clamoured at my legs I released a dozen tits and a toucan, the rumpled falcon who razored away from my shoulders with a cry of disgust. Bending down, I let an ungainly flamingo struggle from my back, extending its long legs like a nervous cripple. The children screamed as it clambered on to my shoulders and took off towards the filling-station. I hid my face, then poppéd a hummingbird from my mouth. In a spectacular finale, I vented the last of the birds from my body, filling the shopping precinct with a torrent of wings and feathers.

Delighted as I was to amuse the children and their mothers, I remembered how I had tried to play Pied Piper in the London parks. Had I, in some way, anticipated that I would one day possess these powers? I wanted to teach these children to fly, capture birds with their bodies, I wanted husbands to merge with their wives, young men with their sweethearts, children with their parents, ready for their last flight to the unseen paradises of the air.

Flying fever swept through Shepperton. Children raced around the shopping mall with model aircraft and badgered their parents to be taken on an aerial jaunt. By the time I reached the war memorial on my way back to the river a procession of several hundred people followed me.

Beyond the memorial the road shelved towards the park. Swept down the incline, the crowd of frustrated children and parents ran after me, pulling at the rags of my flying suit.

'Blake . . . !'

'Stay here, Blake . . . !'

Fighting my way through this mêlée, I clambered over the heads of the children and lifted myself into the air. Three feet from the ground, I moved along at the head of the procession.

'Take us with you, Blake . . . !'

Free to breathe at last, I turned to face them. As I hovered there they clamoured up at me, like refugees fearful of being abandoned in this jungle town.

'Come on! All of you! Fly!'

Two young men in motorcycle jackets jumped up and down in the road, trying to climb on to the air. A middle-aged woman struggled with the sunlight falling into her face, wriggling her hips as if trying to shed her corsets. Below me everyone was shimmying and cavorting, laughing to each other like people attacked by a plague of amiable insects. Only the children watched me with serious eyes. A dozen of them clustered around me, trying to touch my feet.

'Blake, please . . . ' A ten-year-old girl with blond pigtails offered me a sweet as a bribe. I leaned down, took her shoulders and lifted her into the air. Squealing with delight as she held down her skirt, she floated free on the noisy air, leaned over and helped her younger brother into my arms.

Suddenly the air was filled with children. They shrieked happily when they looked down at their kicking feet, already well above their parents' heads.

'Sarah, be careful . . . !' Chasing her daughter with raised hands, an anxious mother left the ground. Legs pedalling furiously, she soared into the air and embraced her daughter, smiling happily as they sailed towards the park.

Followed by the procession, I set off down the road, the head of a huge kite drawing its heavy tail along the ground. Those left behind were kicking and jumping, doing everything to climb on to the air. A young man broke free, then helped his girl-friend up beside him. The old soldier with the shooting stick rose stiffly into the air. Sailing along, he waved his stick at me as if he had already learned a thing or two to tell me about flying.

While we swept forward to the park entire families ran from the side-streets to join us. The sometime executives playing truant for their third day threw away their briefcases to join the tail of the procession, laughingly locked arms and mimicked the high-kicking efforts of the people in front of them, only to find to their astonishment that they too were in the air.

By the time we reached the park more than a thousand people were following me. The last stragglers joined in, film technicians and actors from the studios wearing antique gaiters and goggles, a butcher in a white apron who was giving away the last of his meat to a happy circle of dogs and cats, two mechanics in greasy overalls from the filling-station.

From the door of a telephone booth the village policeman watched us with a look of deep suspicion, obviously debating whether to caution the whole town for a serious infringement of the by-laws, some medieval statute against miscellaneous and indiscriminate flying. Then I heard him shout out, aware that he was alone in Shepperton. He threw away his bicycle and ran after us. Helmet in hand, he clambered on to the air and sailed along serenely at the rear of the procession like the guard of an aerial train.

Last of all came the three crippled children, hurrying down the deserted high street. Jamie jumped and twisted on his iron shackle, as if all along it had been a secret catapult which would propel him into the air. David lumbered behind him, out of breath and too puzzled to explain to Rachel where everyone had gone. The blind girl tilted her head and pressed her hands to her ears, confused by the hundreds of familiar voices over her head, the squeals of the other children falling from the crowded air.

I waited for them to join us, and held up the procession when we reached the park. The policeman and a film actor leaned down to take their hands. With a last effort David climbed on to the air, eyes wide at the sudden lightness of his great head. After him came Jamie, crippled legs pedalling in long and elegant strides. But Rachel, muddled by the shouting voices, swerved in a panic across the pavement and lost herself among the dish-washers and television sets. Before I could help, David and Jamie waved to me and jumped down on to the ground to comfort Rachel.

I was sorry to leave them behind, but already I was looking into the sky and the waiting sun. Like an airliner at take-off, the procession rose into the air behind me, watched by the curious deer feeding among the trees. There were gasps of astonishment when Shepperton fell away below us and the long bend of the river appeared. The swordfish and porpoises, the dolphins and flying fish leapt from the silver water, urging us on our way.

Silent now, we soared in a wide circle three hundred feet above the rooftops. The cool air quietened everyone. Beside me the children sailed along with their faces raised to the sun, hair streaming behind them. Imitating me, they held their arms straight out at their sides, they and their parents, the old and the young with the same rapt expression, sleepers waking from their long dream.

We were soon more than a mile above Shepperton, this jungle town surrounded by its palisade of forest bamboo, an Amazon enclave set down here in the quiet valley of the Thames. The streets were deserted, and everyone was with me, except for the old people at the geriatric unit and the members of my family. Father Wingate stood on the beach among his archaeological specimens, waving his straw hat to encourage me. Mrs St Cloud watched from the bedroom window, still unable to believe her eyes, but delighted for me all the same. Stark stepped from his hearse, unfurling the canopy of a hang-glider as if tempted to join us. Even Miriam, my sky-bride still wearing her wedding dress, stood on the lawn among the eager pelicans, waiting for me to come down from the air and rescue her from these suitors.

Directly above the church I halted the procession and waited for us all to take up our station. Shepperton flew behind me with outstretched arms, the members of a congregation about to worship within the cathedral of my aerial being. Their faces were expressionless, sunk now into an entranced wakefulness. The cool air ruffled the girls' skirts, and flicked at the hair of the small boys. Their parents stared at my shining figure as if seeing themselves within me for the first time.

Nearest to me was the ten-year-old girl who had joined me in the air, her right hand still clutching a sweet. I held her wrists and drew her towards me, holding her gently in my arms.

'Sarah, dear . . . wake now.'

I waited for her to release her breath, which she held tightly for fear that she might slip suddenly and be dashed to death in the empty streets.

Then with a surge of confidence in me she seized my hands and embraced me eagerly. I pressed her against my naked body. The cool air rushed furiously between us, opening a hundred vents to our deaths below. But the sun fused our skins together, and I drew her into my flesh. I felt her heart race within my heart, her little lungs pumping within the great canopies of my lungs. I felt her slender arms, steering me as I reached across the bright air to embrace her younger brother.

'Stephen . . . come here.' I heard her voice speak from my throat.

The boy hesitated, his round face reflecting the sun like

159

a mirror. He threw himself into my chest as if diving into a warm pool. His head pressed against my sternum, his hands searched my hips and stomach, hunting for a doorway into my body. Calming him, I took him into me, swallowing his mouth, his cool lips and sweet tongue, inhaling his hot breath, letting him enter my flesh and pass through me.

Stronger now, recharged by these small spirits, I moved through the procession, beckoning towards me the hundreds of men and women poised in the running air with out-stretched arms.

'Emily . . . Amanda . . . Bobby . . . ' Quickly I embraced the rest of the children who had followed me all day, taking their narrow hips into mine. When their parents watched me anxiously I released the children from my body, disassembling myself like some gentle marine monster exhaling the minnows that had taken up residence within his mouth. They hung around me in the air, waving and smiling when I drew them into me one by one.

I moved on, and touched the shoulders of a young mother whose son I had taken. Her strong body seized mine with an almost violent embrace. I felt her long thighs and hard hips, the sharp bite of her mouth within my jaw. Her bones once more held her son's within the deeps of my marrow.

A mesmerist moving through a sleeping audience, I embraced the rest of them, the old men and women, the husbands and wives, the policeman and the retired soldier, bodies gross and slender, clumsy and graceful. In their eyes, as they held my hands, I saw the same confidence and pride in me. I drew the last of them into me, a young actor from the film studios in his antique flying gear. He embraced me happily, entering my body like a lover.

Alone now in the sky, I moved in huge strides across the air. I had become an archangelic being of enormous power, at last strong enough to make my escape. Far below me the thousands of stranded birds cowered in the airless streets, helplessly flicking their wings at the scattered bank-notes.

160

I hovered above the motorway, ready to land in the nearby fields and abandon my passengers, set down the inhabitants of a complete town in the waist-high corn among the startled farm-workers.

But as I sped northwards through the air a strange gradient turned me against myself. The wind leaned its great back upon me. Every tissue in my body, every nerve and blood-cell held me in their grip as the people within me pulled at my heart with the draw-strings of their affection. A thousand needs and loyalties formed an immense embankment around which we sped in an invisible circle.

Swept back towards the centre of Shepperton, I found myself once more above the deserted streets. Exhausted, I hung passively between the soft bolsters of two gentle clouds. The ground fell away below me. The sky was brightening as we rose through the cool air. I felt the townspeople lying serenely within me, sleeping passengers in this ascending gondola propelled by some profound upward dream. They were carrying me away towards the sun, eager to lose themselves in that communion of light.

Desperate to escape from them before I was burned to death, I rallied myself and dived towards Walton Bridge like a berserk test pilot. But once again I was deflected by my passengers and curved back upon myself. Angrily I swerved away from the solid air. I pretended to climb towards the sun, and then plunged into the empty shopping mall, ready to dash us all against the ornamental tiles, scatter the corpses of myself and these townspeople across the appliances and furniture suites.

The ground rose through the rushing air. At the last moment I again felt the steadying affection of the people within me, a warm hand that steered me safely across the roof of the car-park. Releasing them into the air behind me, I gave up any attempt to escape and brought the huge train down to a breathless stop outside the supermarket.

As everyone happily dismounted from the air I leaned

helplessly against a parked car, like some demented roller-coaster driver who has secretly planned to plunge his passengers to their deaths but is calmed by a friendly child. The entire breathless population of Shepperton was landing around me, led by the shrieking children. The old soldier tottered on unsteady feet, waving reprovingly at the sky with the wrong end of his shooting stick. Giddy housewives pulled down their skirts, young men straightened their hair. Winded, but pink-cheeked, the village policeman sat in an armchair outside the furniture store. Everywhere people were pointing to the sky, whose high vaults were criss-crossed by the vapour trails we had left behind us, elaborate cat's-cradles that stitched the air together into the choreography of an archangelic ballet. I could see clearly the curved wakes that marked my futile attempts to escape, dissolving into the unsettled air above Walton Bridge and the film studios.

Despite my anger, I knew that I was bound to this town, both by the inhabitants' need of me, their growing recognition that I had unlocked the doors to their real world, and by the finite universe of my own self. Yet as I looked at these happy people with their singing skins, smiling and waving to me as they had done high above the town, I knew that if I were to gain my freedom I must first escape from them, from their care and affection.

They moved away arm-in-arm through the quiet streets, urging the frightened birds at their feet to fly again. As they passed me they smiled shyly with the sweetness of lovers who had known the most intimate places of my body. Their chilled skins let corridors of cool air through the humid afternoon.

However, there were no longer as many of them as there had been before the flight. Two windswept mothers searched the now deserted shopping mall, peering into the sky above their heads as if their children still hovered there.

'Sarah, come down, dear . . . '

'Bobby, it's the birds' turn to fly . . . '

I walked past them, naked in the rags of my flying suit. Within me I could feel the bodies of ten-year-old Sarah and her little brother, and of a teenage boy. Jealous of their freedom, I had not released them when we landed. I needed their young bodies and spirits to give me strength. They would play forever within me, running across the dark meadows of my heart. I had still not eaten, although this was the fourth day since my arrival, but I had tasted the flesh of these children and knew that they were my food.

CHAPTER 28

Consul of This Island

The sun was setting fire to the sky. I climbed to the top deck of the car-park and looked out over the rooftops of Shepperton. Below me the vivid forest was filled with thousands of birds, transforming this humdrum town into a tropic paradise conjured so easily from my mind. But over my head the wavering signature of some senile skywriter marked my futile attempt to escape. Whoever had marooned me here had made me consul of this island, had given me the power to fly and to turn myself into any creature I wished, the power to conjure flowers and birds from my fingertips. However, I knew now just how meagre those powers were, as if I had been casually banished to some remote Black Sea port and given the right to make the stones on the beach sing to me.

Was I supposed merely to amuse myself? I watched the unhappy mothers wander away through the late afternoon. One of them stopped to speak to the peacocks sitting on the portico of the bank, asking them if they had seen her son and daughter playing among the clouds. But I could hear their faint voices in my bones.

The last of the townspeople had walked home through the jungle streets. No one had noticed that I was naked, taking for granted that the pagan god of their suburbia, the presiding deity of these television sets and kitchen appliances, would be dressed in nothing but the costume of his skin.

At my feet was the semen-stained suit, this cast-off of the dead priest which the three children must have brought here for me while I took everyone else on our aerial jaunt. Looking down at it, I knew that I would never wear it again. I kicked the trousers and jacket over the ledge into the street below, deciding that from now on I would go naked, expose my body to these people until they at last recognized it.

From that skin came all my powers. The more I showed it to the air and the sky the greater my hope of winning them to my side. I resented being trapped in this small town. Sooner or later, I would have to challenge the invisible forces which had exiled me to Shepperton, pit the resources of my deviant imagination against theirs.

And already I dreamed of extending my small authority to the world beyond Shepperton, to the other towns of the Thames Valley, even to London itself. I almost welcomed the arrival of the television cameras and newspaper reporters. The jungle dusk bathed my skin in a green and gold light, as if my body were being oiled by strange lusts. The streets were lit by the plumage of the scarlet ibis sitting on the roofs like so many exotic lanterns lighting my way. Roused by my will to fight back, I stroked my bruised ribs. I decided to exploit my powers to the full, and if necessary in the most ruthless and perverse ways, perhaps stumble on undiscovered talents that would set me free.

I strolled around the roof of the car-park in the dusk, this concrete ramp from which I had launched myself into the air. I decided not to return to the St Clouds' mansion, but to make my home here in this labyrinth of canted floors.

However, for all my will to succeed, I knew that my time might be running out. I remembered the warning vision of the holocaust. For all my anger, I still wanted to save these people who had first saved me, above all Miriam St Cloud. I was sorry that she was not with me here. I thought of her smile and scent, her scuffed heels and broken nails, a limitless inventory of excitements and possibilities. In some way the key to my escape lay within the common lives of the townspeople of Shepperton. Already I had remade their lives, unsettled their notions of marriage and parenthood, their sense of thrift and pride in work well done. But I needed to go further, to undermine the trust between wives and husbands, between fathers and sons. I wanted them to cross the lines that divided children and parents, species and biological kingdoms, the animate and inanimate. I wanted to destroy the restraints that separated mother and son, father and daughter.

I remembered my bizarre attempt to suffocate Mrs St Cloud, the strange way in which I had tried to rape the little blind girl, and the unconscious young woman I had nearly murdered in her apartment near London Airport. These crimes and lusts were the first stirrings of the benign forces revealed to me in Shepperton. My schoolboy mating with the earth, my attempt to revive the cadaver, my Pied Piper obsession with some nearby children's paradise, had all been premonitions of these powers, which I could share in turn with the people of this placid town.

Thinking of Mrs St Cloud, my adopted mother who had shared my bed, I touched my bruised mouth. Suddenly I wanted everyone in Shepperton to merge together, mothers to mate with sons, fathers with their daughters, to meet within the brothel of my body as they had done so happily in flight.

Above all, I wanted them to praise me, so that I could draw from that praise the strength to escape from this town. I wanted them to praise my breath and sweat, the air that had even briefly touched my skin, my semen and urine, the imprints of my feet on the ground, the bruises on my mouth and chest. I wanted them all in turn to lay their hands on me so that I would know who had revived me. I needed them to bring their children to this labyrinth, to give me their wives and mothers.

Remembering Father Wingate's words, I was certain now that vice in this world was a metaphor for virtue in the next, and that only through the most extreme of those metaphors would I make my escape.

CHAPTER 29
The Life Engine

The day swept on towards a barbarous evening.

From the roof of the car-park I watched the forest canopy closing above the town. Hundreds of palm trees rose from the suburban gardens, their yellow fronds overlaying each other and sealing the rooftops below a vivid tropic blaze. Everywhere the vegetation glowed with an extraordinary luminescence, as if the sun had become a lens and all the light falling through the universe had been focused upon Shepperton.

I smiled into the crowded air, thinking of all the failures in my past life – the police harassment and third-rate jobs, the dreams running off at half-cock. Now an urgent nature was rising on all sides in response to me. Clouds of electric dragonflies and huge butterflies with wings like clapping hands swerved around me. Every leaf and flower, every feather in the plumage of the scarlet ibis standing below me on the roof of the filling-station was charged with a fierce light.

Shepperton had become a life engine.

Around the outskirts of the town dense groves of bamboo and prickly pear sealed off the roads to London and the airport. Half a mile from the station an incoming train stood stranded on its track, unable to penetrate the cacti and palmettos that had sprung between the rails. A line of police vehicles waited at the foot of Walton Bridge, their crews trying to force their way through the bamboo palisades which speared forward as quickly as they were cut back. A fireman with a heavy axe began to hack a path through the stout bamboo. Within a dozen steps he was surrounded by fresh shoots and wrist-thick lianas that laced him into the bars of a jungle cage from which he was released only by the winches of the exhausted police.

By the late afternoon the sun's disc at last touched the forest canopy above the film studios, and the jungle light flowed in a blood tide across the roof of Shepperton. Two helicopters circled the perimeter of the town, a police Sikorski and a smaller machine hired by a television company. Cameras peered down at me, and the sounds of a loud-hailer reverberated through the dense foliage. The Sikorski clattered along the high street, fifty feet above my head, but the clouds of birds rising and falling in the liquid air drove the aircraft back, its crew confused by the hundreds of people waving happily from their gardens. Naked in the rags of my flying suit, I saluted them grandly from the roof of the car-park, this labyrinth and hanging garden from which I presided over Shepperton.

At dusk, when a thousand cerise and cyclamen lights moved through the forest canopy, the flickering plumage of bizarre birds, the first naked people began to move along the streets of Shepperton. As they strolled arm-in-arm down the suburban roads, smiling unselfconsciously at each other, I was sure that they were naked, not because they felt a sudden wish to expose their bodies, but merely because they had become aware that they were clothed. There were families with their children, men with their wives, elderly couples and gangs of teenagers. They sauntered casually through the flocks of orioles that crowded the pavements, and relaxed in the dusk light on the settees outside the furniture store.

Aware of me standing above them on the roof of the car-park, a group of middle-aged women began to construct a circle of small shrines to me in the shopping mall. Outside the supermarket they arranged a pyramid of detergent packs, and assembled a miniature tabernacle from the washing-machines and television sets. Flattered by this show of gratitude, I tore small tags from the scorched fabric of my flying suit and threw them down to these naked women.

Happily they placed the oil-stained rags within the shrines and decked them with flowers and feathers. As the dusk deepened I watched these handsome women move around the centre of Shepperton, building little temples of oil cans in the filling-station forecourt, pyramids of transistor radios outside the appliance stores, deodorant aerosols in the entrance to the chemists. I was proud to preside over them, to be the local deity of the car-wash, the launderette and television rental office. I had graced their modest lives with impossible dreams.

All over Shepperton, as night fell across the jungle streets, people were taking off their clothes. They strolled through the warm air, below street-lights coloured by orchids and magnolia, plucking flowers from the vines and decorating each other's bodies with chains of blossom. Outside the furniture store the old soldier with the shooting stick had thrown away his tweed jacket and trousers. He set up a small booth behind a reproduction escritoire, where he adorned the bodies of teenage girls, dressing their small breasts with flowers. The bank manageress, a naked Juno of the dusk, stood outside her bank among the coins reflected in the coloured lights, handing flowers to the young men who passed by.

The last of the helicopters had retreated into the darkness, taking their noise with them across the reservoirs and poppy fields. The headlamps of the distant traffic lit up the bamboo stockades that surrounded Shepperton. Then, as Mrs St Cloud appeared naked from the shadows of the banyan tree, I knew that I had finally imposed my wayward imagination on this small town. Unaware that I was watching her from the car-park, she walked along the pavement behind a group of adolescent boys, her white body still marked by the bruises of our sex together. For all her heavy breasts and fallen buttocks she had a splendid and brutal beauty.

The centre of Shepperton was filled with hundreds of naked people, strolling to and fro like the crowd on an

169

evening ramble. I saw Father Wingate, naked but for his straw hat, in the forecourt of the filling-station, marvelling at the flowers and birds. As Mrs St Cloud approached he greeted her with a charming salute, hung a lei of myrtle flowers around her neck. When they saw me they waved together to me, smiling like guests in a dream snared half-willingly into some strange game.

But I alone knew that they were naked.

All evening a strong and open sexuality stole through the happy streets, never once revealing its true purpose. As I looked down at these guileless people I knew that none of them realized they were being prepared for their parts in an unusual and perhaps depraved orgy. Already I wanted to provoke the unseen forces who had elevated me to this state of grace.

Husbands and wives separated without ceremony and strolled arm-in-arm with other partners; fathers dallied with their daughters in the leafy arbours outside their houses; mothers caressed their sons as they sauntered across the shopping precinct. A group of teenage girls lolled like amiable courtesans on the divan beds outside the furniture store, beckoning to the men passing by. People wandered in and out of one another's homes, helped themselves to whatever took their fancy, wives decorated themselves with their neighbour's jewellery.

Two people alone remained aloof from these festive games. After dusk, when it became too dark for him to continue his salvage of the Cessna, Stark moored his dredger and returned to Shepperton. Through the late afternoon he had worked the capstan and jib, manoeuvring the pontoon above the submerged aircraft. Giving up for the day, he sat at the wheel of his hearse and roved up and down the back streets of the town, ransacking the houses abandoned by their owners. I watched him load the hearse with rolls of carpet, television sets and kitchenware, an obsessed removal man single-handedly evacuating this jungle-threatened Amazon town. As he drove through the evening throng in the high street he saluted me frankly and without guile. Already his zoo had become a substantial depot of looted equipment, and a gleaming pyramid of dish-washers and deep freezers rose among the cages of the aviary.

I admired Stark, with his dream of appliances, but I was thinking of Miriam St Cloud and waiting for her to wear her wedding dress for me. I was afraid that she too might appear naked in these evening streets. Although I had taken her into my body, felt the knuckles of her bones knock against mine, her vagina clasp my penis, my sexual desire for her had gone, leached away by our flight together. I wanted to embrace her only in the same way that I wished to merge with all the living creatures of this town.

'Blake, will you teach us to fly . . . ?'

'Night-flying, Blake . . . teach us to night-fly.'

The teenage girls lounging on the divan outside the furniture store had crossed the street, their flower-bedecked bodies glaring in the coloured lights. Yet for all their giggles and coyness, even they were unaware of their nakedness. Pushed through the strolling crowd by a party of boys, they waved up to me.

'Come up here,' I called to them. 'One at a time – I'll teach you to fly.'

As they argued with one another, unable to agree who should have the first flight, a woman's voice rang out over the noise of the crowd.

'Emily, now go home! Vanessa and the rest of you, keep away from Blake!'

Miriam St Cloud crossed the street from the supermarket, beckoning the girls away. She had put on her doctor's white coat, buttoned firmly across her blouse. She smiled a hard smile at the naked bystanders, deliberately unshocked by these nude patients assembled here as if for some midnight venereal inspection.

She signalled the girls away from the jungle decks of the

171

car-park, a maze of vines and bougainvilia, and looked up at me with a measured gaze. From the set of her strong chin I knew that she had decided to overcome all her confusions and make a last stand against me. Did she remember that she had already flown with me, and had briefly passed through the gateway of my body into the real world?

The last light of the vanished sun crossed the roof of the car-park. Leaving Miriam to argue with the young women, I went down to the floor below and waited among the parked cars.

'Blake . . . you'll teach me to fly?'

Only a few feet from me, a young man stood naked in the silver darkness. In the street-light reflected from the chromium fenders I could see that his pale skin had been cut by the brambles crowding the staircase and concrete decks. For all his effort, he looked at me sceptically, as if not yet convinced by my powers of flight. I waited for him to approach me, counting the contours of his slim hips and thighs in the darkness.

'Mrs St Cloud told me to come to you. Is this where you hold your flying school?'

I gestured him towards me into the chromium dark. I lusted after this youth. His smell of fear excited me, I could taste his sweat in the darkness, and see the sharp white of his teeth in his uncertain mouth, his pale palms ready to strike me. I lusted after him, but for his body and not for his sex.

'Right – I'll teach you to fly.'

His white skin was dappled like a harlequin's costume by the coloured street-lights. I could see my reflection in the windows of the cars around me, the ragged pelt of the flying suit, the semen pearling on my penis, the goggles on my forehead like scarlet horns.

Taking his hand, I guided him between the cars into the deeper shadows at the rear of the floor. In the back seat of a flower-bedecked limousine I embraced him gently, caressed his nervous skin, pressed his cold hands against the gates of my body.

At the last moment, as I eased him into my chest, he gave a sudden cry of fear and relief. I felt his long legs within mine, the shafts of his bones forming splints around my femurs, his buttocks merging into my hands. His sex melted and dissolved upon my penis, the fontanelles of his skull opened again for the first time since his birth. The mosaic of his cranium sank through the sutures of my head. His grimace with all its terror and ecstasy moved through me like a claw seizing my face. With a last sigh he merged within my flesh, a son reborn into his father's womb. I felt his strong bones anneal themselves to my own, his blood vent its bright tide into my veins, the semen of his testicles foam as it dashed in a torrent against mine.

While he lay within me, his identity fading for ever, I knew that I would never release him, and that his real flight was taking place now across the skies of my body in the rear seat of this limousine. The last motes of his self fled through the dark arcades of my bloodstream, down the sombre cause-ways of my spinal column, following the faint cries of the three children I had taken into me that afternoon.

For a few final seconds he soared within me, as I rode his body through its last night. Riding him, I became an androgyne of multiple sex, an angelic figure raised upon the body of this young man. I embraced him within me as I embraced myself.

CHAPTER 30

Night

Why had the sun not stopped in the sky for me?

All that evening, and through the night that followed, I presided over Shepperton from the heart of the multi-storey car-park. In the dusky streets around me ruled an innocent and open copulation. The entire town mated together, in the leafy bowers that had sprung up among the washing-machines and television sets in the shopping mall, on the settees and divans by the furniture store, in the tropical paradises of the suburban gardens. Hundreds of couples of all ages caressed each other as they tried to teach themselves to fly, confident that through their affection for each other they could regain the air.

None of them was aware of their sex, as innocent as cherubs of what was taking place between them in these jungle bowers. I saw Mrs St Cloud wander happily through the flower-filled streets, her belly smeared with smegma, breasts bruised by the hands of boys. I saw the bank-manageress, standing with a peacock in her arms, offering money to the passers-by. Neither of them knew that they were naked.

Meanwhile I rested in the dark rear seat of the limousine. The body of the young man had refreshed me. My eyes were keener, my senses tuned to a thousand unheard signals that poured from every bird and flower. Since my arrival in Shepperton I had eaten nothing, and I was certain now that my real food was the bodies of these young men and women. The more of them I took within me, the greater would be my powers. I had been imprisoned in Shepperton, not only by the seven people who had witnessed my crash, but by the entire population of the town, and once I had taken them all into me I would at last be strong enough to escape.

Lying back in the flower-decked limousine, I remembered the frightening compulsions that had filled my last years. I had dreamed of crimes and murders, unashamed acts of congress with beasts, with birds, trees and the soil. I remembered my molesting of small children. But now I knew that these perverse impulses had been no more than confused attempts to anticipate what was taking place in Shepperton, my capture of these people and the merging of their bodies with mine. Already I was convinced that there was no evil, and that even the most plainly evil impulses were merely crude attempts to accept the demands of a higher realm that existed within each of us. By accepting these perversions and obsessions I was opening the gates into the real world, where we would all fly together, transform ourselves at will into the fish and the birds, the flowers and the dust, unite ourselves once more within the great commonwealth of nature.

Soon after dawn, as I sat in the rear seat of the limousine, I found a twelve-year-old girl peering down at me through the window. Somehow she had made her way through the labyrinth of the car-park, up the canted floors crowded with brambles and bougainvilia.

'Blake, can I fly . . . ?'

Ignoring the waiting sun, which I left to get on with the task of feeding the forest, I opened the door and beckoned the girl towards me. From her nervous hand I took her brother's model aircraft and placed it on the seat. Reassuringly, I helped her into the car beside me and made a small, sweet breakfast of her.

CHAPTER 31

The Motorcade

The streets were strangely silent. I stood on the roof of the car-park, feeling the sun bathe my skin. A light wind drugged with the scent of mimosa and honeysuckle stirred the rags of my flying suit.

Around me everything was still. The thousands of birds sat on the roofs of the abandoned cars, perched in the gutters of the supermarket and post office, and on the portico of the filling-station. Together they seemed to be waiting for something to happen. Were they expecting me to fly again for them?

Irritated by the silence, I hurled a concrete chip into the flock of flamingos standing around the fountain in the shopping mall. They staggered into each other, flailing their wings in an ungainly pink glare. Then down an avenue of bungalows I saw a small group of people hurrying away below the jungle canopy, like naked conspirators fleeing through the forest.

Petals drifted along the high street under the watching eyes of the birds. I waited for the townspeople to appear. Were they frightened of me, and had they realized at last that they were naked? Had Miriam St Cloud turned them against me, warning them that I was a god reborn from the dead? Perhaps they were ashamed of what had happened between them the previous night, and feared that at any moment I would leave the car-park, and go down among them, seize them as they cowered in their bedrooms and take them into me one by one.

But, if anything, I wanted only to help them.

The first of the afternoon's helicopters hovered over the river by Walton Bridge, its crew crouched over their cine-camera. The palisade of bamboo that surrounded Shepperton was now fifty feet high, a fence of golden spears. All morning the helicopters had patrolled the perimeter of the town, kept back by the clouds of birds driven into the air by their beating fans. As a flock of excited fulmars rose below the circling machine the sound of gun-fire came from one of the deserted streets. A heavy bird fell like a bomb from the crowded sky. Stark ran after it through the groves of young bamboo, nets and shot-gun in hand, blond hair lashed like a pirate's behind his neck. He had abandoned his work on the Cessna and was now openly hunting the birds, following the helicopters as they surveyed the town.

No doubt Stark feared that all this would soon end, that the outside world, the police and the television companies, a legion of sightseers and vandals would break into Shepperton and drive away these exotic creatures before he had prepared himself for them. I left him to his hunt, more concerned with how I could draw the people of Shepperton into a far larger snare. Already I was thinking of my last supper. Once I had devoured everyone in Shepperton I would be strong enough to move into the world beyond, through the quiet towns of the Thames Valley, a holy ghost taking everyone in London into my spirit before I set off for the world at large. I knew that I had defeated the unseen forces who had kept me here, frightened of the unlimited powers I had discovered in myself. I was the first living creature to escape death, to rise above mortality to become a god.

Again I thought of myself as an advent calendar – I had opened the doors of my face, swung back the transoms of my heart to admit these suburban people to the real world beyond. Already I suspected that I was not merely a god, but the first god, the primal deity of whom all others were crude anticipations, clumsy metaphors of myself . . .

'Blake – ?'

Only half-recognizing my name, I turned to find little

177

David squinting at me through the bright sunlight. His shirt and trousers were pierced by brambles, his forehead scratched by thorns as he climbed the stairway. Somehow he had solved the maze of floors and made his way up to the roof.

'Blake . . . Rachel and Jamie want –'

He stopped, forgetting whatever message he had been sent to deliver. Perhaps the little girl had guessed shrewdly that his deformed mind might be the right key to fit the maze. She and Jamie stood in the street below. Ignoring a macaw that screeched at him from the portico of the filling-station, as if urging him to undress, Jamie murmured away to Rachel. With a small hand to her shocked face she listened to his commentary on the barbarous day, unable to believe her ears.

David looked up at me, eyes struggling under his heavy forehead to grasp what I was doing. I could see his concern for me, but I avoided his critical gaze. Did he realize that I was about to leave Shepperton, taking the birds with me, and that he and his companions would be alone in this silent town when the television companies arrived?

His hand touched the ragged waist-band of the flying suit, trying to draw me away from the ledge. Looking down at his small body and deformed head, I felt a surge of pity and affection for him. I thought of taking him with me, merging him into myself with the others. They could play there for ever in one of the secret meadows of my heart.

But when I reached out to embrace him he flinched away from me and slapped his face as if trying to wake himself from a nightmare.

'David, we'll fly now . . . '

As I seized his clumsy head, ready to press it to my chest, I heard a fire-cracker explode in the street below. A dozen voices shouted up at me, there was the sudden clamour of the returning crowd. Releasing David, I looked down into the street. The whole town was reassembling. Hundreds of

178

people streamed towards the centre of Shepperton from the quiet side-roads. They waved up to me, throwing flowers and letting off fireworks. Burned by the sun, their naked bodies had a savage glow.

Now I saw why they had all slipped away to their houses that morning, and what had kept them so busy all day. A party of actors and technicians led a procession through the gates of the film studios, wheeling forward a dozen floats which they had built on to the roofs of their cars.

'Blake!' Their leader, an elderly actor in television commercials, shouted up to me cheerfully. 'We're holding a party for you, Blake! Come down and join us . . . !'

He pointed to the decorated floats, a series of spectacular variations which the set designers and props men had assembled on the theme of flight. Huge papier-mâché and wickerwork constructions, some resembled heraldic birds, immense condors of bamboo decorated with thousands of flowers. Others were pastiche aircraft, biplanes and tri-planes, put together from the mock-up models at the film studios.

The motorcade halted below me, waiting while I left the roof of the car-park and went down to greet them. Heavy with the scent of blossom excited by the late afternoon sun, the air in the street formed a sweet sea on which we all hung as if in a dream.

'They're our tribute to you, Blake. We want to give you something to remember when you leave.' The actor cleared a way for me through the pressing crowd, these naked account executives and shoe salesmen, computer program-mers and secretaries, housewives and children. Happy to see me, they plucked blossoms from their garlands and threw them at me, hoping that my skin would transform them into birds. Everywhere cine-cameras were focused on me, recording the scene.

But I was concerned with more serious matters, intent only on organizing my last day here. I moved down the line of floats, admiring each one in turn. I greeted the bank-manageress and the old soldier, who stood proudly by their creation. Mounted on a taxi-cab of the local car-hire firm, this was the most spectacular of all, an extravagant wicker-work structure with multiple wings, like an eccentric windmill designed to fly simultaneously in all the dimensions of space-time. I liked it immediately, knowing that it was the right one for me.

Everyone waited. Lit by the afternoon sun, a thousand faces were raised to me as I climbed on to the roof of the taxi. Cameras whirred, flash-bulbs flared against the ointment-greased skins. Were they aware that I was about to celebrate my wedding with this town, a marriage to be consummated in a unique way? And that within a few hours they would all have begun a new life in the small suburbs of my body?

I placed my arms in the wing-sockets and eased my temples into the helmet of the headpiece. The huge structure shivered above me, but I carried its weight comfortably on my shoulders. The mouth-strap and harness pressed against the bruises on my lips and chest, and I could almost believe that I had worn this grotesque bird-costume once before when I first flew into the air-space of Shepperton.

Led by the excited children, the motorcade set off towards the river. I sat on the roof of the taxi, holding the head-dress above me. On its great wings and beaked head perched dozens of small birds, tits and wrens and robins, their little faces peeping through the coarse plumage.

The procession had reached the war memorial. Every living thing in the town accompanied me, concourses of birds, packs of dogs and small children, deer leaping among the naked throng following the parade of cars. The light faded. As if nervous of witnessing whatever I intended to do with this small town, the exhausted sun withdrew behind the swathes of carmine cloud that leaked from its disc. A blood light lay over the jungle rooftops, and over the plumage of the flamingos and parakeets, transforming Shepperton into a fever-ridden zoological garden. The same eerie glaze covered the glutted bodies of the fish leaping from the river and the breasts of the young women holding my legs as I stood up on the roof of the taxi.

Above the chittering of the birds I heard a helicopter cross the elms by the river. The blank machine shambled through the fading light. Its clattering fans drove a storm of leaves and insects into the air. Holding tight to the head-dress, I felt the pressure of the helicopter's blades as it veered away and scrambled back towards the river. All over the park, birds were falling slowly from the sky. Losing its purchase on the changing air, the helicopter slid sideways towards the roof of the church, its engine accelerating madly. At the controls the pilot's white hands jerked like a nervous juggler's.

The motorcade halted in confusion. Dogs and deer darted between the wheels of the cars, naked children ran to their mothers, tripping over the pathetic birds that covered the ground. Torn from the wicker wings, thousands of petals formed a boiling cloud around our heads.

'Dr Miriam – get back, doctor!' The old soldier ran forward, waving his stick. I struggled with the head-dress, which was now a powerful glider trying to lift me into the air. Through the whirl of petals I saw that the centre of the park had been transformed into an emergency landing strip. Helped by David, Rachel and Jamie, Miriam St Cloud was setting out a circle of torch-lights on the open grass.

I stepped down from the taxi, tottering below the head-dress. Almost strangled by the mouth-strap of the helmet, I was unable to shout to Miriam as she took off her white coat and waved it frantically at the retreating helicopter.

But I now controlled the air. Followed by the crowd, I ran forward across the petal-whipped grass. Hundreds of naked people ran past me, clearing a way for me and shouting up at the helicopter as the hapless machine was driven back across the river in a tornado of petals. Shreds of bamboo,

181

wicker and lace whirled up into the dusk. The line of floats swayed forward, carried now by the townspeople, as if sailing through a mist of blood.

I felt the head-dress lighten. My feet had left the ground. I was moving again into the real time, taking my congregation with me towards the church. As I sailed along, my arms outstretched in the huge bird-costume, Miriam St Cloud faced me in her circle of light.

'Blake!' she screamed at me above the noise of the helicopter, through the flashes of the camera-bulbs. 'You're *dead*, Blake!'

She tried to protect the children hanging to her skirts, waving her white coat at me as if trying to ward off an approaching devil with whom she would be forced to mate. Alone of the people of Shepperton, she knew that she was about to mate with me for the last time.

The helicopter had retreated to the water-meadow across the river. Swept along towards the church, I saw Miriam knocked from her feet by the running crowd. As she knelt on the grass she was seized by the young women, a group of secretaries who happily stripped the clothes from her shoulders and lifted her into a head-dress of feathers.

Together we soared across the park, borne on a cloud of petals and sailed through the open windows of the church.

Later, I hung naked beside Miriam St Cloud, each of us in our bird-dress, our feet a few inches above the undraped altar. Below us the nave was filled with the worshipping townspeople of Shepperton. Arm-in-arm, they sailed through the air above the aisle, a concourse of embracing figures, delightedly filming each other on this last flight. I was ready now to take them into me, into the host of my flesh. I needed their bodies to keep me in flight, to give me the power to move on to the world at large. From there I would fly on across the planet, merging with all creatures until I had taken into myself every living being, every fish and bird, every parent and child, a single chimeric god uniting all life within me.

Beside me hung Miriam St Cloud, her eyes closed, a dreamer floating in her deepest trance. After our marriage I would know her only as one of the lights in my bones.

I reached out to embrace her for the last time. But at that moment, while I looked into her sleeping eyes, Stark stepped into the entrance of the church, his rifle in hand.

He stared up at the congregation circling the dark air of the nave ten feet above his head, and at the huge bird-costumes which Miriam and I wore on our shoulders. His sweat-stained face was without expression, but he moved swiftly as if he had made up his mind long before. He raised the rifle towards Miriam and myself, and shot us each through the chest.

For the second time that week I fell through the air. At the foot of the altar I lay dying among the feathers of my winged head-dress. Above me swayed the lengthening streamers of my still flying blood.

CHAPTER 32

The Dying Aviator

All night I sat against the altar of that derelict church. Trapped by the head-dress of flowers and feathers around my shoulders, I was unable to move, my legs propped uselessly in front of me. Near me, but beyond my reach, Miriam St Cloud lay face upwards on the stone floor. Her blanched skin, from which all colour had been drained by Stark's bullet, had taken on a nightmare glaze, as if the blood in the delicate capillaries of her cheeks had been replaced by the purulent yellow wax. Shortly after midnight her thin lips parted into a widening gape, a silent rebuke screamed at me by this dead woman doctor.

At first, as we lay side by side in our head-dresses, I hoped that she was still alive. Stark's bullets had passed through our hearts, but I knew now that I would never be killed by Stark or anyone else in this small town. Perhaps my own immunity would carry itself into Miriam. Then through the darkness I smelled the changing odours of her body – the vivid spice of her sweat and the hot kill of her blood faded into the staleness of common death.

All around us were fragments of stained glass, pieces of apostles, saints and sacred animals which reflected the leaping flames of dozens of bonfires. Through the open doors of the church I could see the jungle burning in the warm night air. Thousands of terrified birds cowered in the branches of the banyan tree as the townspeople piled kindling around the roots and set fire to them. All over Shepperton people tore the vines and creepers from the roofs of their houses. They siphoned fuel from the parked cars and doused the palmettos and tamarinds in their gardens.

Throughout the night they roved the town in packs, axes

thrashing at the tropical forest I had so lovingly created for them. I heard the crying of the fulmars, the frightened hooting of the owls, the weeping of the deer. On the wall of the vestry the skeleton of the winged creature trembled in the flames, as if this ancient bird-man dislodged from the river-bed was trying to tear himself from the display case and fly away through the night.

During the hours before dawn the streamers of my blood sank through the air, long tassels that extended from the wound in my chest, gaudy banderillas in a dying bull. Stark's soft-nosed bullet had struck me in the centre of my breast-bone, traversed my chest and exited in a hundred fragments each carrying a piece of my heart.

Although I was still alive, I felt only a numbing despair. I knew that my powers had vanished, and with them all my exaltation of myself, my pride in being the presiding deity of this small domain and of having proved my right to enter that real world into which I had briefly stepped since my forced landing. Once again I had been plucked from the air, at the very moment of my marriage to Miriam St Cloud.

Already I knew that I was guilty of many crimes, not only against those beings who had granted me a second life, but against myself, crimes of arrogance and imagination. Mourning the young woman beside me, I waited as my blood fell from the air.

At dawn a party of deranged aviators arrived.

'Blake! He's still alive!'

'Don't touch him!'

'Call Stark!'

Led by the old soldier with the shooting stick, they entered the church one by one. They pressed their backs to the pillars, frightened that by coming too close to me they might be whirled off their feet into some insane vortex. Their faces were black from the jungle fires, hands raw from the shafts of their axes. They approached timidly, these account executives and bank clerks, hiding behind one another. Having destroyed their clothes the previous day, they were now dressed in costumes looted from the film studios, a motley of uniforms from the air spectacular – antique open-cockpit flying suits, fleece-lined jackets, broad-shouldered airline uniforms.

As they stared down at me, axes raised uneasily in the dawn light, Stark arrived and pushed his way through them. Blond hair loose around his shoulders, he wore the sleek, form-fitting gear of a gunship pilot. He seemed deliberately to be playing a leading part well above himself, the death-angel in a film of aerial Armageddon.

He stood among the fragments of glass and pointed his rifle at me, ready to speed another bullet through my heart.

'You're alive all right, Blake. I know that.' He spoke quietly, in an almost patient tone. 'Anyway, you're not dead – I saw those eyes on the beach . . . '

I could see that he was not wholly convinced I had lost my powers, and half-hoped that I might have retained just enough of my strength to be of use to him in the coming television interviews. I tried to raise my hand, to forgive him for shooting me, but I was unable to move. The pennants of my blood still hung a few inches from the floor, undulating around Stark's feet, kept aloft by the spirits of the children I had taken into me.

Stark turned from me and stared down at Miriam St Cloud. For all the yellow gape of her mouth and the flies festering on her eyelids, the young woman I had loved was still present in the beads of moisture that soaked her hairline, the mole by her left ear, the childhood scar below her chin. Her worn hands were raised to the wound in her chest, and she clutched at the spray of dried blood like a bride clasping an unexpected bouquet of dark flowers forced on to her breast by an uninvited guest.

Stark looked down at her without a trace of pity, as if he had saved the skies of Shepperton from a bird far more dangerous than myself. I realized then that he had killed her because he feared she might have conceived a child by me and become pregnant with some sinister winged creature who would destroy them all.

Spitting on her feet, Stark beckoned the others forward.

'Right – take him outside. But watch him in case he tries to fly.'

At last overcoming their fear, they pulled me from the church. Outside the porch they lifted me on to a metal trolley taken from the supermarket. As they propelled me past the film studios, mock-aviators with a dead colleague in his winged head-dress, the pennants of my blood shivered in the cool air. Stark ran ahead, raising his rifle to the sombre trees, ready to make short work of any bird unwary enough to look at him. He dashed back to me, and pushed aside the old soldier who was prodding my head with his shooting stick.

In a hostile but still deferential way, he murmured: 'We'll take you flying, Blake. You like flying. I'll teach you to hang-glide.'

We moved past the war memorial through the deserted streets. Smouldering vines and creepers lay on the pavements, lengths of charred fuse left behind by a demolition squad who had moved through Shepperton during the night. Thousands of blanched flowers covered the high street, and the wet plumage of slaughtered birds lay among the blood-stained petals. The arms of the banyan tree still hung over the town centre, but a dozen bonfires lit below the heavy branches had carbonized the bark. Trapped within the blackened roots were the hulks of burnt-out cars.

Outside the supermarket a small crowd had gathered, a raw-faced group of husbands reunited with their shocked wives, children with their parents, dressed in a motley of garments salvaged from dustbins and bonfires. They pressed around me, these executives and shop assistants, who only a few hours before had happily sailed with me around the nave of the church.

187

A dishevelled young woman in a soot-stained evening dress struck my face with her sharp fingers.

'Where's Bobby? You took my son away!'

The others clamoured around me, shouting out the names of their lost children.

'He's still alive! Look at his eyes!'

Stark waved them back with his rifle and manhandled the trolley towards the car-park.

'Don't touch his hands! He's a dead man!'

They were stamping on the pennants of my blood that floated from my open heart like the still fluttering tail of a downed kite. The old soldier lashed at them with his stick.

'Don't look at me, Blake! I'll cut your eyes out!'

A chorus struck up among the appliance islands and bedroom suites.

'Cut off his hands! And his feet!'

'Cut off his *penis* !'

'Don't *touch* it!'

Covered with spit, I sat helplessly in the trolley, the tattered head-dress around my shoulders. Stark was peering up at the car-park. I knew that he planned to throw me from the concrete roof, confident that this time I would fall. But did he guess that I would survive, even if he dropped me from his hang-glider?

'Stark, we need him here.' The old soldier held on to the trolley, remonstrating with Stark. 'Without Blake we'll never escape.'

My mind drifted away into my bones, wandering through my exhausted body as they argued. Spittle stung my cheeks and hand, the pennants tore at my savaged heart as hands tugged at them. I had become a maypole idol, stitched together in my own blood by these grimy and excited women.

I woke again as Stark propelled the trolley along the street. We swerved in and out of the gloomy side-roads. All over Shepperton the remains of winged head-dresses lay against the garden fences, as if during the night an aerial armada had been shot down over the town. Wan-faced people squatted in their doorways, lighting small fires of palmetto leaves. Nervous children slashed erratic slogans in the bark of the palm trees.

We approached the bamboo palisade, beyond which lay the open road to London and the airport. Large gaps had been burned through this once impenetrable forest wall, and the first early risers watched from the quiet windows of the neighbouring village, no doubt mystified by this costumed mob pushing along the wounded body of a winged man.

We raced through a breach in the palisade. But as the excited shouts subsided around me I felt once again that sensation I had known on my first day in Shepperton.

'Keep on! Don't give up now! We'll be on the news tonight!' Thumping my head with his rifle, Stark drove on these exhausted executives, their wives and children. One by one they faltered and broke into a dispirited walk. Catching their breath, they looked back at Shepperton, which had now receded from them, a mirage miles away towards the south. Beyond the perimeter formed by the motorway the red-brick houses of the village lay on the horizon, a distant perspective on a Victorian postcard.

Stark threw his rifle across my legs. With a cry of disgust he turned the trolley towards Shepperton.

'You can keep us here now, Blake,' he muttered to me. 'But before it's all over you'll fly again for the television companies . . .'

For the next hour we roamed around Shepperton through the sombre jungle streets. Barely conscious, I sat propped up in the supermarket trolley as this exhausted troupe of suburbanites in their aviators' costumes swerved around the half-empty town. Led by Stark, they charged across the parking lot behind the filling-station, only a hundred yards from the motorway. Shouting hoarsely, they stumbled forward, a shabby light brigade running the trolley over the rough ground, a battering ram they hoped would break through the wall of the world I had placed around Shepperton. But within seconds they found themselves plodding wearily across the largest car-park in the world. The cinder surface extended to the horizon, isolated cars separated by miles of empty parking bays.

Driven back again, we retreated to the town. The post office and supermarket reassembled themselves around us. Determined to prove that his authority over this new time and space was the equal of mine, Stark led us behind the furniture store, where once again we lost ourselves within an endless terrain of furniture suites and kitchen units, archipelagos of appliance islands that stretched to the horizon, as if the contents of all the suburban homes on the planet had been laid out in the infinite sales bay of the universe.

'What good are you, Blake?' Despairing at last, Stark lost interest in me. Leaving his troupe outside the car-park, he wandered towards the banyan tree and began to shoot at random into the branches. Exhausted, the townspeople squatted around me in their aviators' gear, picking at the plumage of the dead macaws that lay among the damp flowers. One by one they drifted off, until only the old soldier with the shooting stick remained. Before leaving, he took the handles of the trolley and propelled me down the high street, left me to collide head-on into the railings of the war memorial.

CHAPTER 33
Rescue

I was alive and I was dead.

All that day I lay in the tatters of the winged head-dress among the yellowing wreaths at the foot of the war memorial. I had fallen from the trolley on to the stone steps, and the pennants of my blood entwined themselves around the obelisk, caressing the names of the men and women from Shepperton who had died in the country's wars. Unable to move, I waited for Mrs St Cloud and Father Wingate to come and bandage my wound, but they had abandoned me. I saw them across the park, Father Wingate comforting the mother as they left the vestry where Miriam lay. I knew that they had decided not to bury her until I had died again.

Meanwhile the outside world seemed to have forgotten Shepperton. The traffic moved along the motorway towards London, the drivers and their passengers apparently unaware of the existence of this small town, as if the mental screen surrounding Shepperton reflected only their own passing thoughts.

Through the humid afternoon a faint rain fell on the smoke-stained houses, dripping from the blackened vines and palmettos. I listened to Stark rove the streets with his rifle, killing the few birds which ventured from their perches.

The townspeople of Shepperton were hiding in their bedrooms, but at dusk a party of women approached the memorial and began to abuse me. They were the mothers of the children I had taken into me, those girls and boys whose distant souls ran through the dark galleries deep within me and alone kept me alive. The women had brought garbage with them in plastic bags. Their aviators' suits torn open to

191

the waist, they pelted me with the wet rubbish and hurled dead birds at me.

For all their hate, I was glad that I had taught them how to fly. Through me they had learned how to become more than themselves, the birds and the fish and the mammals, and had briefly entered a world where they could merge with their brothers and friends, their husbands and children.

I lay at their feet, trapped by the winged head-dress. The streamers of my heart rose on the cold air and fluttered at their faces, the lost spirits of their sons and daughters.

That evening I saw the faces of the three crippled children watching me through the damp light, small moons quietly circling each other. They squatted among the dead flowers and macaws, and played with the pennants of my blood. Rachel fondled them, her blind eyes flickering raptly, trying to read their mysterious codes, cryptic messages from another universe transmitted by the ticker-tape of my heart. David stared gravely at the dying jungle that covered the shop-fronts, puzzled by this pointless transformation. Meanwhile Jamie mimicked me, pressing wet poppies to his chest, squeezing the juice between his fingers. Once he crept forward and placed a dead crow by my head, but I knew that he was not being cruel. I had become a cripple like himself.

Under the cover of darkness the children came to life, and pulled me on to the trolley. Rachel's hands punched my legs, trying to bring them to life.

Fires burned through the dark streets, rising from the upper decks of the multi-storey car-park. The children propelled me swiftly past the deserted clinic towards their secret meadow.

In the grey light I saw the white form of the aircraft they had assembled over my grave.

CHAPTER 34

A Mist of Flies

So the children took me to live in my tomb. I sat like a scarecrow in the flower-filled grave on an upholstery of dead birds, surrounded by the rags of my head-dress still attached to me by the shoulder and jaw-straps. Sections of the Cessna's wings lay in the darkness on either side of the grave, and fragments of the windshield and tailplane formed a crude fuselage. Even the propeller had dislodged itself from the river-bed and been dragged across the meadow. A bent and rusty sword, it lay on the grass at my feet.

The three children sat in the shadowy arbour, deformed cherubs in a mortuary garden. An almost tangible miasma had settled over Shepperton. The trees were covered by a sombre canopy, as if a grey shroud had been draped over the dying jungle. Light no longer streamed from every leaf. The birds remained silent, hidden among the fading orchids and magnolias, whose petals were now as waxy in their death as Miriam St Cloud's cheeks.

Dark wings fluttered like ragged sails above me. Vultures were gathering in the dim sky, landing on the yellow grass to feed off the bodies of slaughtered birds. A small griffon alighted on the propeller in front of me, talons pinioning this two-bladed sword. Everywhere a macabre vegetation was emerging. Strange predators moved through the grass. Snakes climbed from the banks of the creek. A plague of spiders cast webs of pus across the trees, drawing silver shrouds over the dead flowers. Above the grave white flies festered in a halo. As a pale dawn filled the meadow I could see shrike attacking the last of the hummingbirds and impaling them on the thorn-bushes.

The whole of Shepperton was sickening, poisoned by the

despair flowing from me. Soon after dawn the three children returned. Hoping to revive me, Jamie for the first time brought a live bird to me, a bruised robin which he released through the grass. Too frightened to approach me, the children crouched in the lice-filled grass. Jamie hooted plaintively to himself and ducked his head below the circling vultures who waited to feed on my corpse, that flesh from which they themselves had sprung. David placed his hands across Rachel's eyes, concerned that even her blindness might not save her from these horrors.

A few people wandered along the pallid streets, still dressed in their aviators' costumes. Through me a town of pilots was dying, and through them I in turn was dying.

Yet I was still alive.

In the centre of the park the vultures were feeding on the carcases of the deer. A dark clutch of the raptors sat on the fuel pumps in the filling-station, while their leader devoured a dead dog. A grey wind stirred the thousands of crushed flowers as people backed away from the birds, watching them wanly from the doorways. Armed with knives and garden forks, they stared across the park, where the grass was covered with dying deer. A single stag stood weakly among his exhausted herd.

I waited for the police to come and rescue me, eager now to admit that I had stolen the Cessna. But the world had lost interest in Shepperton, as if an invisible screen had been placed around this small town. The last of the police cars had driven off, and the crews of the television transmission vans were packing away their equipment.

That afternoon no helicopters flew.

From the dead elms I heard voices raised. Led by Stark, a party of hunters returned from an expedition to the river, dragging a bloody porpoise across the dead flower-beds. Through the shabby rhododendrons I saw Stark's excited face and fraying hair. Covered with blood, he hung the fish on a hook outside the butcher's shop by the war memorial.

As the hungry housewives scurried in from the side-streets Stark stood on a metal barrel and cut steaks from the porpoise's flesh.

All afternoon the slaughter on the river banks continued. The damp grass in the park was slick with blood and scales as the dolphins and porpoises, the groupers and salmon were speared by a gang of killers working from Stark's pontoon, bloody aviators revenging themselves on these creatures of another element. Stark waded waist-deep in the water and beat to death the white swordfish as it tried to hide in the drowned Cessna. I felt the last light of its spirit call to me in my tomb.

That afternoon blood ran through the flowers and feathers in the streets of Shepperton. Greedy for food, the townspeople thronged the butchers' shops, shouting for the raw meat which loaded the counters where Stark and his aviators gave away my flesh.

Ferociously buzzing insects filled the grave, carrion wasps destroying their own wings in their greed for the dead birds. A mist of flies fled from my skin and descended on the living and the dead.

CHAPTER 35

Bonfires

Snakes slid backwards across the sombre meadow. Birds flew upside-down through the dying trees. Ten feet from my grave a starving dog hunted for its dung, squatted on the ground and reabsorbed it hungrily.

My blood lifted from my open heart in black crepes, streamers that trailed through the darkening forest. A strange fungus coated the feeble trees, feeding on the nitrogenous air. A foul miasma hung over the park and deformed the dying blossoms. I sat in the aircraft in a cockpit of dead birds. On all sides I was surrounded by a garden of cancers.

Death ran out of me into the quiet meadow, and through the streets of Shepperton. I listened to the faint cries of the townspeople as they hunted the forest, shooting the last of the birds.

In the late afternoon a small stag entered the arbour and tottered on skeleton legs towards the grave. It stared at me with wavering eyes, unable to focus the image of my dissolving face, and lay down in the dark grass. Watched by the vultures in the branches above my head, other animals began to gather around me, the last survivors of the little paradise I had brought to this town. A spaniel bitch appeared among the poppies, then crouched whimpering by the Cessna's propeller. The aged chimpanzee I had fed when Stark abandoned his zoo squatted in the grass, striking its head as if to jolt the real world back into the meadow. Last of all, the marmoset rustled along the ground, climbed on to the fuselage and stared at me with huge eyes through the broken windshield.

They were waiting for me to make them well, I who had

laid the streets with flowers and fed them with breadfruit. Unable to move, I sat in the cockpit of the grave. My frozen veins were pencil leads in my arms. The exhausted sky was lit by bonfires as the townspeople tried to burn the jungle from their shops and houses.

I saw the members of my family, ghosts on a dreamed lawn, watching me from the St Clouds' mansion. Father Wingate stood on the blood-soaked grass in an immaculate cassock. But his face and arms were gaunt, and I knew that he had been starving himself to protect his body against me. The three children were with him, Rachel standing asleep with her head on David's shoulder. In the open window of my bedroom was Mrs St Cloud, her pale face wasted on to its bones. She wore her grey nightdress like a shroud, as if she had left her sick-bed to ask me to die.

Even Stark had taken his place in a gondola of his Ferris wheel. A brace of macaws in a gaudy garland around his neck, he gazed at the rusty pontoon moored above the Cessna, stained with blood that seemed to have leaked from the aircraft's cockpit.

They were waiting for me to die and set them free. I remembered the holocaust I had seen as I stepped from the aircraft, a vision of my own death under a bonfire sky. Despite all my efforts to prove myself, I was now a corpse propped in its tomb.

The spaniel snuffled closer to me, trying to take from me my last strength. The chimpanzee lay on his side in the grass, eyes fixed on me. Ignoring them, I listened to the shrieking of the raptors. Somewhere close to me was the shifting of a vulture's wings. I looked across the river, hoping that a helicopter would come to save me.

Despairing at last, I decided to die.

CHAPTER 36

Strength

Even as I was dying I felt a surge of strength. A hand had clasped itself around my heart. Gently it squeezed the ruptured chambers, easing a brief flow of blood through my vessels. My skin warmed, blood seeped again through my frozen capillaries.

For the first time I was able to lift my right arm. As I reached out to the vulture on the branch above me, inviting it to feed on my flesh, I felt the hand press again on my heart. Then I saw the face of the old chimpanzee, and the darkness in his open eyes. At the moment before he died I felt again a surge of life in my chest, as if his heart had been transplanted into my own. I sat up, my chest drumming to this strange heart-beat. I saw the deer's legs give their last kick and I felt my pulse quicken as this dying animal's blood was transfused into my arteries.

I looked down at myself, naked in my ragged flying suit. My skin had lost its ashen tone. When I lifted the head-dress from my shoulders the pennants of blood broke away from my scars and fluttered off through the shabby poppies.

My wound had stopped bleeding. One by one the animals were dying in the grass around the tomb. Each was giving something of itself to me, its blood, its tissues, a vital organ. I felt the chimpanzee's heart beat strongly within my chest, I felt the deer's blood rush through my empty veins, spring flood through a maze of parched conduits, I felt the marmoset's lungs draw the air through my mouth, I felt the spaniel's dim brain at the base of my own, faithful beast carrying her wounded master.

Together they died around me in the grass, surrendering

their own lives for me. I stood up in the cockpit of the grave. Once again I had freed myself from the aircraft.

The forest was motionless. Every activity had ceased, the leaves and grass suspended in silence. I could feel the life flowing into me from all sides, willed to me by the smallest creatures and the lowliest. Together these simple beings were remaking me. The sparrows and thrushes passed their miniature retinas into my eyes, the voles and badgers within their burrows gave me their teeth, the elms and chestnuts willed their sap to me, grave wet-nurses running their milk into my body. Even the leeches on the propeller of the aircraft, the worms under my feet, the myriad bacteria in the soil were moving in a huge congregation through my flesh. A vast concourse of living beings crowded my arteries and veins, transforming the mortuary of my body with their life and goodwill. The cool moisture of snails irrigated my joints, I felt my muscles eased by the flexing of a thousand branches, my flesh balmed in the warm capillaries of a million sun-filled leaves.

I walked across the meadow, surrounded by a strange haze of light, as if my real self was diffusing through the air and lay within the bodies of all these creatures who had given part of themselves to me. I was reborn within them, and within their love for me. Every leaf and blade of grass, every bird and snail was pregnant with my spirit. The forest felt me quicken within its tissues.

I was born again from the lowest of the creatures, from the amoeba dividing in the meadow ponds, from the hydra and spirogyra. I was spawned by amphibians in the creek beside the meadow, and in the river as a dogfish from the body of my mother-shark. I was dropped by the pregnant deer on to the deep grass of the meadow. I emerged from the warm cloaca of birds. I was born by a thousand births from the flesh of every living thing in the forest, the father of myself. I became my own child.

CHAPTER 37

I Give Myself Away

The forest was bright again. Vivid blossoms shone out among the once sombre trees. A familiar light moved through the leaves, as if the divine gardener who supervised this dimmed paradise had suddenly arrived after a late start to his day and switched on its lights. A flying fish leapt from the river, a silver flint that rekindled the day.

At the entrance to the meadow the three children knelt in the grass, their small smiles among the waving poppies. They seemed exhausted but content, tired by the struggle of willing their strength to me, some small part of their deformed bodies – David, perhaps his stoicism; Jamie his excitement in everything; Rachel her curiosity and calm.

The whole of Shepperton seemed to be resting, as if after an immense effort. The townspeople were no longer trying to destroy the vegetation and sat on their doorsteps, axes and saws discarded. Quietly they watched the forest revive.

Everything waited for me. I looked down at my chest, at the healed wound. Even the scar had vanished. Within my breast I felt the organs given to me by all these creatures. I carried a thousand lungs and hearts, a thousand livers and brains, a thousand genitalia of every sex, potent enough to populate the new world that I was about to enter.

I was certain now that I could escape from Shepperton.

I crossed the car-park of the clinic. On the terrace of the geriatric unit sat the old people, the cripples and the senile. The three children followed me, faces lowered to the ground, aware that I was about to leave them. A frown puckered David's massive forehead while he tried manfully to decide on their future. Rachel's face had shrunk in on itself, eyes closed as if she refused to risk the possibility of sight at this time of goodbyes. Only Jamie kept up his spirits. He hooted at the air over his head, testing the sky in the hope that it might send him another aviator.

An old man on the sun-terrace raised his hand, waving to me for the last time. An elderly woman ravaged by leukaemia smiled from her cot, thanking me for the flowers in the garden, the vivid plumage of the birds.

Out of affection for the children, I went back to them. Kneeling in front of them among the parked cars, I took Jamie's hands. I waited until his nervous hoots subsided and his eyes were fixed on mine. Through our clasped fingers I let flow into his body the strength and suppleness given to my legs by the dying deer.

I released his hands. Staring into his eyes, I struck the shackles from his legs. Jamie gasped at his knees, amazed by his sturdy legs. Laughing to himself, he swayed playfully, pretending to fall over. He gave a last whoop, dismissed the sky and ran off across the park, leaping over the flower-beds.

All the while, Rachel listened intently, turning her eyes to the excited grass, unable to read its scurrying codes. Frightened, she backed away from me, releasing her hand from David's shoulder. But then, in a sudden access of courage, she ran forward and seized my knees. She held me tightly, trying to return to me the strength that had flowed into Jamie.

I took her head in my hands and pressed it against my thighs. I touched the dead windows of her eyes. Through my fingers I passed to her the sight of the hawks and eagles, the sure judgment of the condors. Her eyeballs raced under my fingertips, as if she were rapidly dreaming through all the lost sights of her childhood. I felt the quickening nerves rise from her brain like the stems of an orchid, and blossom into the gentle petals of her retinas. Exasperated with herself, she happily tossed her head from side to side, overwhelmed by the light pouring into the dark chambers of her skull.

'Blake, yes ... !'

She pulled away from me and stared wide-eyed at the meadow, at the sky and the leaves. She gazed up at me in a level way, and for a brief moment saw her lover and her father.

Jamie darted between us, swerving among the cars, and then danced around David, who stoically stood his ground, pleased for his friends but unable to understand what had happened to them.

Quickly, knowing that I would soon leave, Rachel took David by the hands and pulled him briskly towards me. I held his massive head against my loins. I felt his strong heart beating, nervous that its role might be taken over by some cerebral usurper. Through the sutures of his skull I passed small slivers of intelligence, thin torch-beams that pierced the dark lumber-room of his brain. As his mind responded, it felt its own way in the ebbing shadows, remaking its broken looms. Last of all I gave him understanding, the good sense of the old fish and the wise snakes.

His head reverberated against my loins, a humming planetarium filled with an astronomy of dreams. He pushed himself away from me, and then looked up with dignified calm.

'Blake, thank you ... Can I help *you* ?'

Courteously, he moved away, strolling shyly between the dusty cars as if embarrassed by this alert and clear-minded tenant who had taken up residence in his head.

Dazed by these efforts, and aware that my mind and body had paid a price for them, I decided to leave. At any moment the first sightseers would flock into Shepperton, followed by the police hunting for the downed Cessna. I rested against Miriam St Cloud's red sports car, remembering the young doctor and the help she had given me after my arrival. In the dust around the door were the marks of her fingers, a last coded message to me.

David was waiting for me. My vision had faded, but I

could see his clear blue eyes watching the old people on the sun-terrace.

'Blake, before you go . . . ' He spoke in an almost adult voice. 'Would you say goodbye to them?'

Following this calm and dignified boy, I walked across the car-park to the terrace. From their cots and wheel-chairs the old folk waved to me, glad to be out in the sun. As I looked up at these moribund beings, sitting here in the doorways of their own deaths, I was tempted to turn and run, fly off for ever across the trees. I knew that if I once gave to them that strength passed to me by the birds and plants I would never be able to flee from Shepperton.

Again I was about to be trapped here.

David waited for me, smiling reassuringly as I began to tremble. He could see how angry I was with these old people, and was leaving it to me to choose whether or not I helped them.

'Thank you again, Blake.'

I climbed the steps to the terrace. One by one I moved among the elderly patients, taking their worn hands. To the old woman with leukaemia, a smiling and ashen bundle, I gave my blood, passing on the gift of the deer and the elms. I held her tiny hands, and the blood flowed into her through the hoses of my wrists. As David beamed with delight, she revived before our eyes. Her warm fingers squeezed my elbow.

'I'll ask the nurse to bring your make-up case, Mrs Sanders.' Laughingly, David separated us and moved me to the next patient. To this old man with senile dementia I gave a second part of my brain, that which I had taken from the hawks and eagles. His lolling head steadied in my hands, his eyes stared at me with the dawning light of a sleepy chess-player waking to see a winning move.

'A few more, Blake.' David steadied me as I moved along the wheelchairs. To the infirm and arthritic, to the diabetic man and the schizophrenic woman I made the gifts of reason and health. My sight blurred as they clambered from their chairs and sick-beds, and clustered around me in their dressing-gowns. A demented old man pummelled my shoulder, grasping for the first time the logic of time and space. The schizophrenic woman trilled some odd song to a nearby tree. The youthful bloom of an adolescent girl suffused her lace-like skin, as if I had transformed her into her own grand-daughter.

David calmly steered me among them as I handed out the gifts of sight and sense, health and grace to these crippled people, dismantling pieces of my mind and body and passing them to anyone who clutched at my hands.

Last of all, to a man with cancer of the mouth, I made the gift of my tongue.

'Blake, you've been kind . . . ' Although David was at my right hand, his voice seemed to come from the far side of the park. I was unable to speak.

Happily, I gave myself away.

CHAPTER 38

Time to Fly

Alone now, blind and almost deaf, the tongue missing from my throat, I shuffled through the busy streets, holding the crutch handed to me by one of the old men I had cured. I was aware of the people of Shepperton around me, and I knew that they were happy at last. Strangely, I was glad to have given myself to them, to have passed on those qualities lent to me by the birds and the snakes and the voles, by the smallest creatures in the soil, lent to me in the same way that the universe had twice lent my life to me. I *had* escaped from Shepperton, by submerging myself in their bodies, leaving myself in the pink bloom of the old woman's skin, in the bright eyes of the once senile old man.

I tapped the ground under my feet, aware that I was standing near the supermarket. But none of the people around me were strangers. I knew them all, their weaknesses and strengths, the smell of their sweat, the blemishes on their backs, the caries in their teeth. I was their mother and father, they had passed through me, born from my aerial flesh.

I reached the filling-station and rested among the fuel pumps. A scent of tropical blossom bathed my skin. I could feel footsteps approaching, hard points on the concrete forecourt. As I crossed the street to the shopping mall, tapping my way with the crutch, others followed me silently, through the derelict shrines among the appliance islands, past the used-car lot to the open ground by the motorway.

I stopped and listened to the steady breathing around me. Was a party of assassins following me, about to stone me to death? I was ready to give them whatever they wanted, my weak legs and arms, my windless lungs, my unmagic loins.

Having stripped me, they would leave a clutch of sightless bones in the motorway dust.

A hand touched my shoulder. I felt someone's warm breath on my neck. Fingers explored my wrists, searching for my pulse, others touched my face, caressed my bruised chest, stroked my blind eyes. People crowded around me, their hands on my body, on my legs, massaging my thighs, lifting my scrotum. A woman's sweet mouth pressed against my lips. I was about to be smothered by all this affection, a deformed baby deliberately suffocated by loving relatives.

A tidal race flowed through me, a violent eagre rushed into my empty blood vessels. The air began to clear. My loins came alive in the hands of the young man who held my penis. His semen recharged my testicles.

'Blake . . . ! Open your eyes!'

Father Wingate and Mrs St Cloud were smiling into my face. Like everyone else around me, they were dressed in aviator's costume, members of a party of Victorian aerial enthusiasts. The priest took off his panama hat and sailed it away over the abandoned cars, then embraced me affectionately.

'Blake, you came through . . . !' All the self-disgust had left him, and his face was unlined, lit by that same interior light I had seen shining through the X-ray photographs of my skull. He seemed gay and light-headed, a young curate enjoying some excellent joke over the communion wine.

Mrs St Cloud held my cheeks in her hands and kissed me on the forehead. As she smiled at me I could see her daughter's expression in her face. Her features had lifted, climbing the bones of her chin and temples. Her blond hair hung loosely around her shoulders.

'Blake, it's time to fly. We're all ready for you now.'

Through my still half-opaque eyes I saw that hundreds of people had gathered around me. They were all there, figures in a white dream glimpsed through that powdery light. All of them seemed younger now, children returning to their

206

earlier selves. There were the bank manageress and the furniture salesman, the supermarket cashiers, account executives and secretaries, the retired soldier and the television actor who had built my winged head-dress, the old and the crippled who had thrown away their crutches and wheel-chairs. Only the children and Miriam were absent. Far away Jamie and Rachel ran across the park, chasing the birds and butterflies. Even David was moving away from me. As he returned to the river he paused by the war memorial to look back at me with his wise smile.

My eyes cleared, and I felt the hands of Shepperton press against me. Each of the townspeople passed something of himself into me, a token of his spirit pinned to my heart as if I were the groom at my wedding.

'Blake! Come on! It's time to fly!'

'Look up, Blake!'

Father Wingate shouted to me, his strong head raised to the sun. Already the first people were rising into the air, the bank manageress and the television actor. They beckoned me to join them, their hands reaching down to take mine. Soon everyone had left the ground. They circled around me in the warm sunlight, their feet kicking the dust into a huge cloud. Looking up at them, I could see their affection and concern for me. Father Wingate, his arm around Mrs St Cloud's waist, floated past me, his knees brushing my shoulder.

'It's time, Blake!' Ten feet from the ground, they flew around me hand in hand, willing me into the air. At last I felt the air cool my bruised toes. I threw the crutch away, and drawn by the force of their love for me, I rose into the sky.

CHAPTER 39
Departure

Holding one another's outstretched hands, we moved together through the sky, an immense aerial congregation. Far below us the town had begun to blossom again into the brilliant forest that had dressed the roofs of these suburban houses. The warm wind carried a hundred scents, and we floated on a perfumed cloud. Happy to be together, we formed a circle around Shepperton, our faces lit by the welcoming sun.

Before leaving for the last time, we decided to give thanks to this small town. On either side of me were Father Wingate and Mrs St Cloud, an enthusiastic young couple delighted with their first flight. We soared through the air beside the motorway, no longer concerned that the drivers in the cars streaming towards London were unable to see us. We hovered above the concrete post across which I had tripped when I first tried to escape from Shepperton, and held a small service of thanks to the stones in the field. We gave thanks to the appliance islands and bedroom suites, to the fuel pumps in the filling-station and to the rusting car which had once sheltered me.

'Goodbye, Blake . . .' Mrs St Cloud had released my hand and began to move away from me, an excited teenage girl in her adult flying costume.

'Bye, Blake . . . !' a child called out, one of the supermarket cashiers now little more than ten years old.

'Blake . . . ' Father Wingate held my shoulders, his slim adolescent face like a spirited novice's. We embraced each other for the last time, and when I released him I could feel his youthful smile linger on my lips.

But already I knew that I could not go with them. I had

taught them to fly, by guiding them through the doors of my body, and now they would make their own way to the sun. Meanwhile others still remained, the three children, the birds and the deer, the voles and the insects which had given themselves so generously to me. Only when I had sent the last living creature on its way towards the sun would I be free to leave.

Already they were a hundred feet above me, a party of happy children moving hand in hand towards the illuminated sky.

'Blake, goodbye . . . '

The last of their voices faded. Alone in this small sky, I sank downwards through the quiet air. I stood on the roof of the car-park, exhausted by the work of sending the people of Shepperton on their way, and looked out over the deserted town. I now knew the meaning of the strange holocaust I had seen from the cockpit of the Cessna as I sat drowning in the river, a vision of the illustrated souls of the people of this town whom I had taken within me and taught to fly, each a band of light in the rainbow worn by the sun.

CHAPTER 40

I Take Stark

I walked along the deserted street, seeing my reflection in the windows of the supermarket. Overrun by the silent forest, the quiet roads stretched past forgotten swimming-pools and empty driveways. A water-spray rotated across an ornamental pond, and children's toys lay abandoned by the garden gates. On all sides the birds crowded the rooftops and telephone wires, jostled for a place on the parked cars. They watched me, waiting for the last act that was about to follow, uncertain whether I would leave them alone here. The condors gazed at me with their ancient eyes, great wings raised to still the air.

'Mrs St Cloud . . . ! Father Wingate . . . ' They had gone to join the sun. But had Stark escaped? Only Miriam remained, lying in the vestry at the church.

'Miriam . . . ! Dr Miriam . . . !'

Above the film studios helicopters were circling. I turned my back on the supermarket. The stains of my semen covered the silent glass, pearls cast among the discount offers. As if inflamed by my last flight, the bruises on my mouth and chest had become glowing coals in my skin.

When I reached the war memorial I could hear the three children playing happily in their meadow. I crossed the car-park of the clinic and walked through the grass towards them. The light from my body flared against the poppies, turning the red petals to gold, lighting the plumage of the condors who followed me from tree to tree.

For a few moments I watched the children, wishing that they could play for ever in this secret meadow. They skipped towards me, crowding excitement into every second. Jamie whirled around my legs, escaping from Rachel's quick hands. He squealed as I picked him up and embraced him.

'It's time to leave, Jamie . . . '

He stared at me in surprise, then seized my shoulders. His small mouth kissed my cheek. He leaned back, let out a final ironic hoot at the world and fell against me. He sank easily through my golden skin, his strong legs kicking for the last time.

Without hesitating, Rachel came to me. Her neat hands separated the glowing grass as if she were housekeeping in the meadow and meant to keep it tidy for the next tenants. She stepped up to me and gravely embraced my waist.

'Time for us all to leave, Rachel . . . '

I took her strong hands, felt her impatient mouth on my own, her tongue feeling my teeth. With a last happy cry she slipped away into my heart.

Alone now, David waited in the long grass. Below his great forehead, his eyes watched me calmly.

'I'll teach you to fly, David. People will be here soon – you won't want to stay when they arrive.'

'I'm ready, Blake. I'd like to fly.' He smiled at his hands, doubting whether they would ever become wings. He showed me an old shoe-box, in which he had caught two Amazon moths.

'I've started to collect them,' he said matter-of-factly. 'It's worth keeping a record of all this.'

'Do you want to catch another?' I asked him. 'I'll wait for you.'

He shook his head, then laid the open box on the grass. We watched the moths flutter dustily through the poppies, insects of gold lit by my skin. David came towards me. He leaned his huge head against my waist, taking a last look at the meadow, at the trees and birds.

'Blake . . . goodbye!'

He seized my hands. His large head, with its open sutures, passed into me, his strong shoulders merged with mine.

211

I rose into the air, and released them to the sky above the park. Like dreamers in flight, they sailed away hand in hand, their faces lit by the welcoming sun.

My skin glowed, so brightly now that the deep grass around me and the dark leaves of the rhododendrons were almost white. I walked towards the river, an archangel moving among the mortuary birds, the light from my body flaring against the trunks of the elms.

I approached the St Clouds' deserted mansion. Hundreds of fish leapt from the water, eager to take my light briefly to their bodies, unhappy that I might leave them behind. Beyond the white water Stark stood at the balustrade of his amusement pier. He had taken off his flying suit and had slung his rifle over his naked shoulder. Surrounded by the birds, the pelicans and fulmars, he watched me as I walked across the lawn. When he threw his rifle into the water I knew that he had given up all hope of challenging me. He listened to the helicopters, accepting that they moved through a different sky.

The dredging platform had broken from its moorings and run aground on the mud-flats along the opposite bank. However, Stark had at last dragged the drowned Cessna on to the beach. The skeleton of the aircraft, with its broken wings and gutted fuselage, lay half-submerged across the sand below the St Clouds' lawn. The once white skin was covered with rust and algae, stained by oil leaking from the engine.

Stark waited for me to approach the Cessna and look into its cockpit. Ignoring the aircraft, I stepped on to the beach and strode along the sand. I climbed the ladder on to the rusting pier. My glowing skin gilded the unicorns, overlaying Stark's paintwork with an even more brilliant patina.

When I reached Stark he stepped back from me. Flinching, he hid his face, as if asking for a few last seconds to prepare himself for death. Then, seeing that I had no intention of hurting him, he raised his hands in a gesture of surrender.

We grappled briefly among the painted gondolas, Stark's strong arms trying to hold me away. Desperately he looked down at the river, tempted to plunge into the calm water. But he would never reach the safety of the Walton shore. He knew that Shepperton was closing around us, and that he was sustained here only by my presence.

'Blake . . . ! I raised the aircraft for you!'

I felt him merge into me, our bodies embracing with the intimacy of wrestlers long familiar with each other. At the last moment he looked up at the funfair and the painted gondolas of the Ferris wheel, an adolescent boy eager to ride the sky.

I flew away to the cool, uncrowded air above the film studios and released him towards the sun.

CHAPTER 41

Miriam Breathes

Alone at last, I made my way along the beach to the wreck of the Cessna. Standing on the submerged starboard wing, I looked through the fractured windshield into the cabin. As I had guessed, the figure of a man in a white flying suit lay beside the controls. Thousands of fish had picked the flesh from his face, and algae hung in grey veils over his empty eyes, but I recognized the skull in the ragged flying helmet.

This drowned flier was my former self, left behind when I escaped from the Cessna. Half-submerged, as if between two worlds, he sat at the controls. Out of pity for him, I pulled back the cockpit door and reached down to his skeleton. I would bury him on the beach, let him take the place of that fossil bird-man, my forbear from the Pliocene, jerked from its long sleep by the crashing aircraft.

I lifted him easily, a clutch of bones in the rags of a flying suit whose missing portions I now wore myself. I felt a profound pity for this dead creature, all that remained of my physical being from which my spirit had broken free. I held this earlier self in my arms like a father carrying his dead son, warming his bones for the last time before I laid him to rest.

Then, as if revived by me, the bones stirred in my arms. The spine stiffened against my chest. The hands clutched at my face. The bony points of the skull struck my forehead, the notched teeth cut against my mouth.

Repelled, I tried to hurl the skeleton on to the sand. Struggling together, we fell backwards into the water beside the submerged tailplane of the Cessna. Excited by his memories of the cool stream, the skeleton fought his way past

214

my hands, his bony mouth clamped against my lips, trying to suck the air from my lungs.

As his brittle ribs merged with mine, as the clinker-like wrists pressed through my arms, I realized then whose mouth and hands I had tried to find since my arrival in this small town. The bruises were the scars of my own body clinging to me in terror as I tore myself free from that dying self and escaped from the drowned aircraft.

Lying on my back in the water, the white hull of the Cessna beside me, I calmed my dead self, taking my bones into me, my shins and arms, my ribs and skull. Around me were thousands of fish, jewelling the sun-filled water, the small creatures who had fed on the flesh of my body as it lay for seven days on the river-bed.

Reaching out, I beckoned them towards me and took the fish into my hands, absorbing once again within myself the fragments of my dead flesh which they had carried like a pearl-treasure within their tissues.

I stood on the beach beside the Cessna. The rising tide swilled around the aircraft, submerging its wings. Although I was now alone in Shepperton, apart from the dead young woman in the church and the congregation of the birds, I no longer felt abandoned here, as if the now annealed halves of myself formed a complete tenancy of this small town.

I left the beach and crossed the lawn below the deserted mansion. A peacock sidled up to me, rattled his tail and waved me towards the church. I watched the birds crowding the rooftops. They had gathered here from all over Shepperton, like an eager audience waiting for the last entry of a matador.

I entered the churchyard and walked through the graves to the vestry. The bright flowers that had sprung from my sex rose around me, their red spears as high as my shoulders, running to seed here among the dead. I stood in the doorway and looked down at Miriam's body, lying on a glass display

215

case in the centre of the vestry. The light from my glowing skin flared against the walls, illuminating the spines and knuckles of the ancient bones of the winged man.

I tore the last rags of my flying suit from my waist and threw them to the floor. I remembered Miriam caressing the young blossoms outside the clinic, urging them to press their heads against her thighs, as if she were trying to seduce the meadow. She now seemed little older than the three children she had looked after, her mouth and cheeks as soft as they had been in life.

Naked, I stood in front of her, and let my glowing skin warm her as I had warmed my dead self on the beach. I thought of the creatures who had given their lives for me, the deer and the old chimpanzee. Holding Miriam's shoulders, I willed into her body everything I had been given, my first and my second lives. If I could rise from the dead I could also raise this young woman.

I felt the life run from me. My skin faded, its light dimmed. Around me the vestry grew dark again. For the last time I gave myself away. Now I would have only enough strength to send Miriam on her way before I returned to the bone-bed on the beach.

I felt her stir. Her right hand rose and touched my face. 'Blake . . . ! You woke me – I fell asleep here!'

CHAPTER 42

The Unlimited Dream Company

'Blake, can't we stay? It's so beautiful here!'

We stood arm-in-arm among the brilliant flowers in the churchyard. Laughing to herself, Miriam raised her hands to the bright sun.

'A little longer, Blake?'

I watched her happily as a flock of hummingbirds hovered about our heads. Miriam had stepped from the vestry with the strong stride and lively gaze of an enthusiastic schoolgirl. The two days of death had made her younger, as if she were visiting this parish church from a newer and fresher world.

Delighted to see me, she stood naked beside me among the headstones. I was glad that she no longer remembered her death. She held my waist in a sudden gesture of affection. 'Where is everyone? Mother and Father Wingate?'

'They've left already, Miriam.' I led her through the graves to the gates of the churchyard. 'Stark and the children, everyone else. The whole town has gone.'

She looked up at the sky, smiling at the rainbow around the sun. 'Blake, I can see them – they're all there!'

Already I was steeling myself against her departure. I knew that she would soon move on to that world of which Shepperton was merely a brightly furnished but modest antechamber. I held her naked shoulders against my chest, breathing the hot scents of her body, counting the small blemishes on her skin, the point of dry wax in her ear. I wished that I could spend forever here among the flowers with this young woman, dress her hair with garlands sprung from my own sex.

But the birds pressed around us. They stood on every window-ledge, and crowded the roofs of the film studios.

Again I felt that the town was closing upon itself, forcing the birds into an ever smaller space. Already the great condors were looking upwards ready to seize their places in the sky.

'Miriam, it's time for you to leave.'

'I know, Blake. You'll come with me?' She touched my forehead, as if taking my temperature, an adolescent girl playing at being a doctor. Each minute she stayed she seemed to grow younger by a year.

She knelt down between the graves and lifted in her hands an infant thrush, a bundle of stippled feathers with a lolling head, exhausted by the strange air.

'Blake, will it be strong enough to fly?'

I took it from her, charged it briefly with my strength, the wing-span of the frigate-birds that filled my arms. As it spread its wings on my hands I felt the gathering vortex around us. A miniature tornado was sweeping the church-yard. The red-tipped blossoms thrashed us with their soft spears, urging us into the air. Miriam struggled with her hair, which rose above her into the swirl of petals. A whirlwind of feathers circled the churchyard, driven around the headstones by thousands of wings.

Everywhere the birds were lifting into the air. As Miriam swayed towards me I gripped her hands.

'It's time, Miriam! Time to fly!'

We embraced, each taking the other's body. I felt her strong bones and firm flesh, the affectionate pressure of her mouth on mine, of her breasts in my breast.

'Blake, take them with us! Even the dead, Blake!'

Together we merged with the cloud of creatures that now filled the sky above the churchyard. We sailed through the vivid air, climbing the long aisles of the sun. We invited the birds to join us, welcome guests at the wedding-feast of the air. We moved in and out of ourselves, a concourse lit by the plumage of the birds, an armada of winged and feathered chimeras that soared above the rooftops of the deserted town.

As the distant traffic moved along the motorway I released Miriam from me and dressed her with the wings of the albatross. In turn she dressed me with the beak and talons of the condors.

On all sides an immense panoply of living creatures was rising into the air. A cloud of silver fish rose from the river, an inverted waterfall of speckled forms. Above the park the timid deer ascended in a tremulous herd. Voles and squirrels, snakes and lizards, a myriad insects were sailing upwards. We merged together for the last time, feeling ourselves dissolve into this aerial fleet. Taking them all into me, I chimerized myself, a multiple of all these creatures passing through the gateway of my body to the realm above. Concourses of chimeric beings poured from my head. I felt myself dissolve within these assembling and separating forms, beating together with a single pulse, the infinitely chambered heart of the great bird of which we were all part.

At last, near the end, the dead rose to join us, conjured from their graves in the churchyard, from the warm soil of the park, from the dust that lined the empty streets, from the damp streams and forgotten burrows. A grey miasma rose from the ground, an aerial shroud that seemed about to blight the trees and the sky, but was then lit by the lanterns of the living beings above it.

At the last moment I heard Miriam call out. She moved away from me, a diadem-gate through which all these creatures passed towards the sun, the smallest and the highest, the living and the dead.

'Wait for us, Blake . . . '

I stood on the beach, the remains of my ragged flying suit lying on the wet sand at my feet. Although I was naked, my skin was still warmed by the creatures who had passed through my body, warming each cell as they crossed its hearth. Looking up at the sky, I could see the last glow of light moving towards the sun.

Shepperton was silent now, abandoned by the birds. The empty river touched my feet, a calm sleeper nudging me in its dream. The park was deserted, the houses empty.

The Cessna was almost submerged, its wings tipping below the sweeping tide. As I watched, the fuselage turned and slipped below the coverlet of the water. When the river had carried it away I walked across the beach to the bone-bed of the winged creature whose place I was about to take. I would lie down here, in this seam of ancient shingle, a couch prepared for me millions of years earlier.

There I would rest, certain now that one day Miriam would come for me. Then we would set off, with the inhabitants of all the other towns in the valley of the Thames, and in the world beyond. This time we would merge with the trees and the flowers, with the dust and the stones, with the whole of the mineral world, happily dissolving ourselves in the sea of light that formed the universe, itself reborn from the souls of the living who have happily returned themselves to its heart. Already I saw us rising into the air, fathers, mothers and their children, our ascending flights swaying across the surface of the earth, benign tornadoes hanging from the canopy of the universe, celebrating the last marriage of the animate and inanimate, of the living and the dead.

J.G. Ballard

High-Rise

Within the concealing walls of an elegant forty-storey tower block, the affluent tenants are hell-bent on an orgy of destruction. Cocktail parties degenerate into marauding attacks on 'enemy' floors and the once-luxurious amenities become an arena for technological mayhem . . .

In this classic visionary tale from the author of *Crash*, *Empire of the Sun* and *Cocaine Nights*, human society slips into violent reverse as the inhabitants of the high-rise, driven by primal urges, recreate a world ruled by the laws of the jungle.

'Ballard's finest novel . . . Vibrant with irony and images, a triumph of artistry and feeling.'   *The Times*

'Harsh and ingenious . . . *High-Rise* is an intense and vivid bestiary, which lingers unsettlingly in the mind.'

MARTIN AMIS, *New Statesman*

'An eerie glimpse into the future. A fast-moving, spine-tingling fable of the concrete jungle.'   *Daily Express*

'A gripping read, particularly if you like your thrills chilly, bloody and with claims to social relevance.'   *Time Out*

'Ingenious, chilling . . . Ballard is a prophetic writer.'

Sunday Times

ISBN 0 586 04456 6

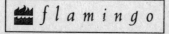

J.G. Ballard

A User's Guide to the Millennium

Essays and Reviews

'Few writers can write with equal facility about Elvis Presley, Norwegian lobsters and Deng Xiaoping. Ballard does so with great flair and energy in this fabulously diverse collection.'
Independent on Sunday

The ninety pieces of J.G. Ballard's non-fiction writing collected here for the first time were written between 1962 and 1995. Many touch on themes and obsessions familiar to readers of his fiction; all show the insight, wit and distinctive vision of the modern world that have characterised his work throughout his distinguished career.

'In a shrinking world increasingly bereft of original imaginations, J.G. Ballard stands alone, a bizarre visionary maverick. Cinema, surrealist painting, crime, the future, madness, sf and China – these are Ballard's specialist subjects. Best of all in this eccentric, relaxed, always readable collection are his laconic wartime memories, the treasure house he kept locked for forty years.'
Irish Times

'Ballard surveys our "cosmic madhouse" like a colossus. Sardonic but never cynical, his range is a delight, from Dali to Walt Disney and Howard Hughes.'
The Times

'Fizzles with subversive intelligence . . . Across an astonishing range, his ironic slant is ceaselessly stimulating.' *Independent*

ISBN 0 00 654821 0

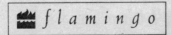

J.G. Ballard

The Crystal World

Through a 'leaking' of time, the West African jungle starts to crystallize. Trees metamorphose into enormous jewels. Crocodiles encased in second glittering skins lurch down the river. Pythons with huge blind gemstone eyes rear in heraldic poses. Most people flee the area in terror, afraid to face what they cannot understand. But some, dazzled and strangely entranced, remain to drift through this dreamworld forest: a doctor in pursuit of his ex-mistress, an enigmatic Jesuit wielding a crystal cross and a tribe of lepers searching for Paradise . . .

In this *tour de force* of the imagination, the acclaimed author of *Crash*, *Empire of the Sun* and *Cocaine Nights* transports the reader into one of his most unforgettable landscapes.

'Of all the unknown regions Ballard's imagination has opened up, this crystalline forest is the most haunting, with its golden orioles frozen in a lattice of jewels and men like conquistadores embalmed in diamond armour. The creation of the crystal world is something magical and not to be missed.'   *Guardian*

'Beautifully rendered . . . Ballard the poet in full ecstatic blast.'
                                                ANTHONY BURGESS

'By far his strongest and most individual novel . . . *The Crystal World* is a powerful dream, impossible to paraphrase.'
                                                BRIAN ALDISS

'Ballard transports us once more into his own mystical, glittering and poetic universe.'   *Sunday Telegraph*

ISBN 0 586 02419 0

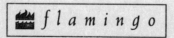